Gabriel - God's Hero
Book 1

GABRIEL
THE WAR IN HEAVEN

ELLEN GUNDERSON TRAYLOR

PORT HOLE PUBLICATIONS
Polson, Montana

First Edition - August 2004
ISBN 0-9700274-8-6
Copyright 2004
All rights reserved
Printed in the United States of America

Cover art by Edward Burney, London 1799

✠✠✠✠✠✠

To My Father
HERBERT EDMOND GUNDERSON
Who Now Walks With Angels

✠✠✠✠✠✠

✠✠✠✠✠✠

How art thou fallen from Heaven,
O Lucifer,
Son of the Morning!

Isaiah 14:12

✠✠✠✠✠✠

✠✠✠✠✠✠

CONTENTS

✠✠✠✠✠✠

✠ ✠ ✠ ✠ ✠

ILLUSTRATIONS

Note: One of the adventures of authoring GABRIEL - THE WAR IN HEAVEN came after I had completed the actual writing. I discovered several works of art related to Milton's PARADISE LOST that fit perfectly with scenes from my book. Since these works are in the public domain, I felt comfortable making a few minor alterations, to fit with my own depictions, and the captions on the prints are from my story. The original artists are all English and French, from the Romantic Period. I trust that they will add to the enjoyment and meaning of this tale, as I have told it.

✠ ✠ ✠ ✠ ✠

A NOTE TO THE READER

Writing about angels must be one of the greatest challenges an author can face. Very few people have ever seen angels, and the Bible is elusive in revealing much about them. Writing about heaven is an even more daunting task. Not only are there few accounts available regarding its description, but none of us will know, for sure, what heaven is like, until we go there. Finally, all attempts to describe God, himself, are bound to be full of quagmires. How does one describe pure spirit, without bordering on blasphemy?

Yet, I was faced with all these challenges when I sat down to write this volume.

I do not claim to be a theologian (an expert on God) or an angelologist (an expert on angels). I have never seen heaven, except in my heart and my "sanctified imagination." I am grateful to those whose writings I have read, who speculate on the scriptural allusions to these topics. Passages such as Isaiah 14:12-15, Ezekiel 28:12-15, Ephesians 6:12, Revelation 12:4, 7-9, and Jude 6 (to name a few) are open to interpretation and full of mystery. You might want to read them in conjunction with this book.

I am also grateful to those daring souls who have told their own stories of encounters with angels or visits to heaven, in so-called near-death experiences or in times of spiritual "ecstasy" and visions. Which accounts are true and which not, only God knows. But from ancient times until the present, godly people like St. Paul, St. John, Augustine and many others have given credible testimony to heaven's reality and to encounters with divine beings.

Regarding difficult matters with which I have had to contend in this book, I have taken the records of Scripture and these respected testimonies, and have blended them with my own hunches and imagination to create a realm which I hope you will embrace. Before you launch out on the adventure of this book, I want to explain how I have rationalized my approach to several sticky issues.

First of all, TIME: It is said that there is no "time" in heaven. Yet, we know that heaven has a history and a future, and therefore, it must be governed by some sort of sequential structure. While heavenly time is not the same as earthly time, I have chosen to tell this story within a time framework, not only because there is no other way to tell it, but because there is no other way that mere mortals might understand it.

Relative to time is SPACE: While heaven is a "spiritual" realm, and spirits are not confined by dimensions, we are told that there are layers to heaven (Paul visited the "third heaven"). We are also told that there are activities in heaven and that heavenly citizens live in "mansions," which implies some sort of spatial structure. Therefore, I have chosen to describe things in terms of space, distance, and dimension, for the same reasons that I use time as a framework.

Next, DAILY SCHEDULE: While we are told that there is no night, and that there is no need for a sun in heaven, there must be periods of rest, for we are told that even God rested after all his labors. We also know that Lucifer's name means "Son of the Morning," so I deduce from this that there was a dawning to God's heavenly creation. It follows, that there might be ebbs and flows to the heavenly calendar: dawn, day, evening, and the like. While many people might prefer to spiritualize all of this, for the sake of storytelling, I have not.

And then there is a host of other matters, more or less important, which required authorial decisions: LABOR, FOOD, BODIES, ANIMALS, and so on.

I depict the entities of heaven as

involved in many creative LABORS: music, praise, industry, manual work. The incredible notion that heaven's citizens do nothing for eternity but play harps and float on clouds is not at all biblical, nor is it attractive. I believe that a Creator God made all his creatures to be creative themselves. This divine spark is seen everywhere, especially in human beings. How could it be less so in heaven? All humans, and surely all angels, are gifted with various talents and callings. St. Paul tells us that there are varying castes among the angels, varying degrees of power and authority. There are also different professions: warrior angels, worship angels, guardian angels, and a host of other angelic workers are mentioned in Scripture. Why would there not be builder angels, teacher angels, chef angels, even writer angels?

The Bible does not tell us that when we go to heaven we become angels; humans are humans, angels are angels. However, I do believe that our callings here on earth are but a foreshadowing of what we will enjoy in heaven! And I also believe that our angelic superiors have their own callings and interests.

Did I say "chef" angels? This brings us to the question of FOOD. Do angels eat? If so, how do they process their food? I was delighted to find that there is a reference in the Psalms to "angels' food"! Of course, we know that there will be a "marriage supper" in heaven, when all of the redeemed are gathered there. The food itself must be so pure, and heavenly bodies so efficient, that there is no waste, all fuel burned completely and perfectly.

But what about BODIES? Oh my, what does one say about "bodies" in heaven? Well, we know that, while heaven is a spiritual realm, angels are visible from time to time. We know that at the last trumpet sound, when the "dead in Christ" shall rise, they shall be given new bodies. Therefore, I deduce that, while heaven is spiritual, angels and all the citizens of heaven must have some sort of amazing containers. Certainly they are more changeable and accommodating than ours, allowing the angels to take on various forms for various tasks. But, I cannot imagine an angel throwing his crown at God's feet, if he has no head on which to wear it, and God has no feet at which to throw it!

Sub-note to the issue of BODIES: Are there are sexes in heaven? While we know that there is no procreation, that is not to say that there is no variety. While the Bible only records encounters with "masculine" angels,

God is compared to a "mother hen" and Christ to a female sheep. Apparently both masculine and feminine traits exist in heaven.

Next, ANIMALS: I am not *dog*matic on this, but I cannot imagine a fabulously exciting and endearing place that has no animals! We are told, in fact, that Christ will return on a white horse, that the Spirit took the form of a dove at Christ's baptism, and so on. As some have said, "If there are no dogs in heaven, I don't want to go there." Be that as it may, I have elected to populate Gabriel's heaven with a plethora of beasts: furry, feathered, small, large, and eminently helpful. If earth is but a poor shadow of heaven, animals must be even more companionable there, than they are here.

The UNIVERSE: You will find that, in my story, I allude to planets outside of the heavenly domain. These planets I have existing before the creation of earth. What I am referring to are the planets and universe which were very possibly in existence before our solar system (the earth, stars/planets, sun, moon of Genesis) was ever created. Who is to say that God had not enjoyed eons of creative achievement long before he decided to form our world and populate its sky with other spinning and burning fragments? And, yes, I have the pre-earthly universe populated with life. Do we believe we are the only souls he ever loved?

And finally, WAR: How can I even suggest that there was a war in heaven? How could a perfect realm know sin, heartache, pain, or suffering? Well, dear reader, it is not I who suggest this, but the Bible tells us, in no uncertain terms, that "there was a war in heaven," that Jesus "saw Lucifer fall from heaven," that Michael fought "the dragon," and so on.

The concept of an angelic rebellion is feasible when we consider that free will is fundamental to all God's thinking creatures. The angels made their choices eons ago, once and forever. We, likewise, must choose to love or not to love the Father.

I am sure there are other mysteries I have not touched on in this Note to the Reader. I hope that this introduction has started you thinking, already, about what the heavenly realm might be like. Whether or not you agree with my suggestions, I trust that GABRIEL - THE WAR IN HEAVEN will bless you and expand your appreciation for a God so great that we will spend eternity learning about him.

In Christ,
Ellen Traylor

PROLOGUE

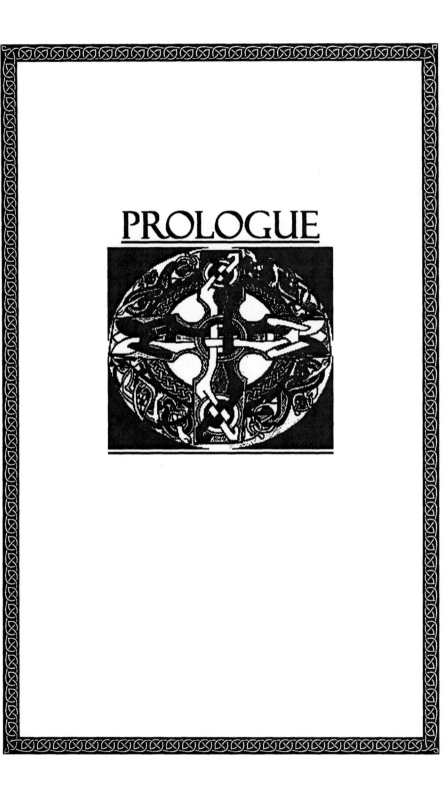

 etween massive columns of an alabaster promenade, the most magnificent of God's creations stood surveying the heavenly kingdom. From this vantage point, he could see to the very entrance, three full valleys away. The eternal light of the inner sanctum spilled out from the portico behind him, throwing his shadow across a radiant, curving stairway, whose foot was lost to sight in the densely wooded gorge below.

As he had left the chamber and entered the veranda, a countless host of beings had fallen prostrate before him, the enormous sentinels who guarded the entrance to the throne room and the eternal worshippers who always lined the stairs' sweeping banisters.

"Hail, Lucifer, Son of the Morning!" they cried out, over and over. "Full of wisdom, perfect in beauty!"

This sort of praise was reserved for only two castes of beings in all of heaven: God Almighty in his three facets, and Lucifer, himself. The only difference between the adulation Lucifer received was that those who bowed to him did not cast their crowns at his feet. That gesture was reserved for God and his Son.

Even Lucifer fell before God. Even Lucifer

removed his diadem and placed it reverently at the foot of the Father's throne.

But, no one else beneath the Almighty was quite so splendid as Lucifer. Not the cherubim who guarded the holy courts, not the seraphim, whose music ebbed and flowed incessantly through the highest chambers.

It was said of Lucifer that he was "sealed with perfection." Even the Father and the Son considered Lucifer their most magnificent achievement.

So did he.

And why should he not? Though he was not nearly so tall as the guards at the entrance to the throne room, he was far more beautiful. Thick dark hair fell in waves to his shoulders, piercing dark eyes saw through all about him with an intelligence unequalled among all his brethren. His body moved with a grace endowed like none other, as though God had taken more pains with his design than with anyone else's. Every muscle, every tendon, every heartbeat was a wonder of glory.

Folded tastefully behind him were his wings, so fabulous that they were often engaged to conceal the Son as he left the throne room, or as he rode out from court in his chariot. At those times, only the Son received more attention than Lucifer, even though hidden from view by his spectacular escort.

When the Son chose to go out publicly, riding on his fabulous white horse without the concealing cover, the praise he received was beyond anything Lucifer ever expected to experience. On those occasions, Lucifer, along with all the lesser inhabitants of the heavenlies, fell before him, casting their crowns alongside his path.

But, in the general life of the palace, Lucifer was the Son's closest companion. Except for the other members of the godhead, Son of the Morning was his dearest friend.

As Lucifer stood, now, upon the balcony, his mind was a swirl of new impressions, his heart full of unfamiliar emotion. He had just come from a meeting with the Father, the Son and the most illusive of the godhead, the Spirit. He had so recently been in the inner sanctum, that the jewels of his fabulous robe were still warm from the heat of the brazen altar, the "stones of purging" that sat in the midst of the holy court.

He did not know what to make of the command he had just received. He knew he was not being demoted. The Father had assured him of that. But, he had been told to descend to the lowest level of heaven, where he was to take charge of a new caste of beings - a tiny, select corps of angels, who would, in turn, be given charge over some new, unnamed project.

"Bring them hither," the Father had said. "Do not reveal the fullness of your glory to them. They will learn it soon enough. All things in their time."

Very well, he would comply. The mystery, the lack of knowledge, made him uncomfortable, but, the very thought of not complying with anything the Father asked had never crossed the threshold of his mind.

His hands trembling, he reached for the clasp at his neck and loosened his cloak from his shoulders. Pulling it before him, he folded it reverently and draped it over the balcony rail. His face twitched as he did this, and he ran his fingers lovingly over the garment, which was the emblem of his prestige and power. Given to him by the Father on the day he was created, this cloak had never been far from him. Wherever he went, he wore it, taking it off only when he dined or when he was at ease within the palace.

Now, he was to leave it behind, going out on a nameless mission.

A gasp of amazement and incredulity escaped his worshippers, at his strange action. What could he be thinking, to strip himself of this emblem?

Lucifer shook himself, straightening his shoulders and lifting his chin. He smoothed the front of his purple tunic and adjusted the heavily gilded belt at his waist. He would keep his dignity, despite the questioning eyes all about him.

As he descended the stairway, the onlookers again bowed themselves in adoration. "Stand up!" he commanded them. "We will have none of this again, until I am restored to my glory!"

Astonished, the worshippers stood up, keeping their eyes averted.

This moment, however, Lucifer did not care what they thought. He struggled within himself as another, more familiar twinge of unease tingled up his spine. He could not recall just when he had first experienced this strange sensation. It had hit him often of late, though its first titillating hint had been in a past so distant, he could not pinpoint its origin.

It haunted him when he had just been in the presence of the Son. It came upon him when he left the throne room and stood upon this very spot, where he was received by his admirers.

He had tried to determine its meaning, but, once, when the meaning had come close to revealing itself, it had so distressed him, he had cast it from him. Surely, it was not what it seemed!

There was not even a name for what it was, he assured himself. Therefore, it was not real. If he did not name it, perhaps it would go away.

But, it did have a name, which teased at the

edges of his mind. It was wrapped around any thought of the Son, so that the love he had for him was sometimes strangely dimmed.

He knew in his heart of hearts that this was *jealousy*.

He knew in his heart of hearts that this was jealousy.

CHAPTER 1

ar away, on a green hillside near the entrance to Heaven, another being took his first breath.

His first thought, which would forever be his first memory, burst forth as word and light. He became in that instant, not as a babe becomes, not as a child becomes, but as a completed being.

He would never fully distinguish between that word-light and the Father. To him, they would forever be one and the same. For the unutterable word was a knowing, not a sound; and the light was creation, the Creator, and it called him into existence as it had always called forth all things.

At that moment, he, himself, was indistinguishable from the word, the light. It would only be much later that he would realize he could be separate from it, if he chose.

Although he was entire in an instant, awareness grew gradually. The knowledge of his own nature began as he opened his eyes and raised himself upon one elbow from the velvety ground where he reclined.

The first thing he saw was his own right hand, its thick, sinewy fingers spread out to brace his weight. He knew the hand was beautiful. No one need tell him so. The knowledge of beauty was part of his make-up, and would remain a part, always. Finely etched beneath the sheen of his skin, the muscles of his hand and wrist moved, rippling as he rocked himself forward to study them. As he bent down, his other hand swept across his body, meeting the first and stroking it in awe and wonder.

His arms, he realized, were glorious for strength. Power and strength, as well as beauty, were intuitive to him. That his entire body was a marvel was instantly perceived. Legs, feet, abdomen, chest, neck, back…all were charged with an urgent need to act, to produce, to…What was that yearning? To serve!

He was sitting erect, now, absorbed in the fact of himself. He lifted his hands to his face and studied the palms, the intricate, fine-grained swirls of the skin pattern, the tips of the eager fingers, the pulse beneath the thinner skin of the inner wrist.

Yes, there was a rhythm to his being, a coursing, repetitive surge that had begun with his first breath. Initiated by the bursting light, that pulse would persist for all of eternity to come, the beating of his heart which would last forever.

He was immortal. But, this fact was not astonishing, for he had no concept of endings.

Enjoyable as his self-absorption was, he did, at long last, become aware of things beyond himself. This awareness first came to him as sound, persistent and growing, a sound that had been with him from his first moment, but which only now gained his undivided attention.

It was a moving sound, a throbbing, surrounding sound, like that of his own pulse, should he rest his head again upon the ground and listen to the thrumming of his heart inside his ears. It arose from a great distance, but was also everywhere around him. He knew, immediately, that this was music. It was also the throb of life itself, forever emerging, growing, expanding across space. Yet it was composed of individual voices, giving it a liquid essence, like that of rushing water.

In fact, there was a river in the distance, licking the shore of the shining highland on which he sat. It was smooth, reflecting a light that seemed to permeate everything, yet to also hover above it all. And spread out across the slope, leading to the river, were others like himself, just arising, as he was, into the knowledge of their own being.

Some of the sound he heard was this stirring of these new lives, the sighs of amazement that they all emitted. But, the choral music of the surrounding sound came from a shore across the flood, from fabulous creatures, tall and slender, arrayed in robes so white they were nearly blinding. These beings, though different than himself and those nearest him, must be related, nonetheless. All of them were kin, he knew, the ones on this side and the ones on the farther side of the river.

As he compared the distant ones to those nearby, he saw that his companions, like himself, were of sturdier appearance, big and brawny, as though built to exemplify strength. They were arrayed, not in brilliant white robes like the beings across the river, but in garments of metallic substance - silver, bronze and even gold cloth. These garbs reached to the knee, and across their chests his cohorts wore vests of heavy mail.

He had not thought, until just now, to analyze his own clothing. It was, as he expected, like the garments of those near him. Upon his feet were heavy sandals, whose laces bound thick leggings about his shins and calves. And next to him, upon the ground, were arrayed a sword and a shield. The shield bore strange designs, swirls and knots of the cleverest art, and in the midst of these were graceful figures, which he took to have some meaning.

As he sat pondering the interpretation, his attention was caught by a marvelous being who wandered among the crowd, as though looking for someone. This character was somewhat larger than himself, and of such impeccable beauty it was hard to imagine he was real. Although he was of similar build to himself, this glorious creature was endowed with marvelous appendages, feathery, fan-like limbs, which lay folded against his back.

As the first studied these amazing features, he twisted his arm behind himself and felt for anything similar. To his astonishment, he could feel the rudiments of feathery limbs jutting out from the folds of his own clothing.

Suddenly, the newcomer was beside him, looking down upon him with a kindly expression. "Yes…you, too, have wings," the being said, noting his inquisitive look. "They should grow in time."

The first blushed a little, and turned his eyes toward his armor.

"And, you have an amazing shield," the visitor noted, as though determined to strike up a conversation.

The first cleared his throat, seeking his voice. "It seems all of us have," he at last replied, gesturing to the thousands who were gathered on the hillside.

With a patient smile, the newcomer explained, "Ah, yes, but not all of them have those letters upon their shields."

"Letters?" he asked. "These are words, then?" He stared at the figures that were woven through the center of the intricate design. "But, I do not read."

The newcomer gave a gentle laugh. "Of course you do!" he said. "Look again. You know what it says."

Suddenly, as he studied the figures once more, they seemed clear as light. *"Glory to the Lord,"* he read.

"That's it!" His new friend chuckled. "It's not so hard, is it?"

"But..." he shook his head, "I did not see it before."

"It all comes of its own accord," the visitor said. "I have been here somewhat longer than you, and I have learned that the Father lets each of us comprehend at his own pace."

As the younger still stared at the shield, the other gestured to the ground. "May I?" he asked.

Scooting aside a bit, he nodded. "By all means! I would like the company."

"Your name?" the visitor asked.

"Name?"

A brief silence passed, as the newcomer waited.

"Oh, of course. I know...The Father has named me *Gabriel*," he replied.

As he realized his name, which seemed to have come to him on the very air, his skin tingled. Speaking it for the first time, he felt his heart race.

The visitor was not a little impressed. *"God's Hero,"* he interpreted. "My, my! The

Father must have great plans for you, Gabriel!"

The younger sat up straight at the endorsement. "It would seem so," he agreed.

"But, then," the elder said, glancing around at the dazzling beings congregated as far as the eye could see, "he must have great plans for all of you."

Gabriel surveyed the crowds. "I take it that we have different purposes…those across the way and those of us gathered on this side?"

His new friend nodded. "There are many different assignments to be fulfilled. Those across the way, for instance, are made for music. They have been singing all day, as you on this side have been emerging."

Gabriel was amazed. "All day? Well, it is lovely. I could listen to them forever." Then, looking at the others, he asked, "And what of us? All of us on this side? Are we made for some sort of action?"

"So it would seem," the visitor said. Frowning a bit, he seemed bemused. "Your tools are made for conflict, though I have never seen conflict in heaven."

Gabriel leaned forward and picked up his shield. Cradling the heavy implement on his lap, he ran a finger over the etched letters. "You say there are only a few of us who have these words upon our armor?"

"I have seen only three others, down near the shore," he said. "I have not spoken with them yet. I do not know their names."

Neither, Gabriel realized, did he know the newcomer's name. "And what are you called?" he quickly inquired.

The great being held his head high. "The Father saw fit to create me before my fellows," he replied. "I was born at another dawn, and so I am called *Lucifer*."

Gabriel was duly humbled. *"Son of the Morning!"* he interpreted. "That is a proud name, indeed!"

Lucifer shook his head. "Pride is not something I care to be associated with," he objected. Then, touching the letters on Gabriel's shield, he added, "We all have but one real duty, you and I and all of us. We were made to bring glory to the Lord."

CHAPTER 2

abriel felt a little shaky as he stood to his feet for the first time. His companion, Lucifer, lent a hand as the younger angel hefted himself to a fully upright position and stood wobbling as he got his bearings.

"Thank you," Gabriel said.

Lucifer's face bore a look of urgency. "The feeling will pass," he assured the younger one. "I did not have anyone to help me stand up. I did not know if I would make it, until I saw the Son standing nearby. A mere look at him, and I was infused with strength!"

"The Son?" Gabriel said. He thought perhaps the understanding of who this was would dawn on him, like his own name had done, or like the meaning of the letters on his shield. But it did not.

Lucifer gave him a penetrating look. "When you see him, you will know who he is. No one will need to tell you."

Gabriel would have inquired further, but Lucifer's sense of urgency seemed to be growing. Gripping Gabriel's elbow, he encouraged him to begin walking.

"Come, we must be going," Lucifer said. "We have been summoned to meet with the

Father!"

Somehow, Gabriel needed no explanation of just who the Father was. He knew, instinctively, that the Father was the Prime Force, the Originator, the Author of all things, the Nameless One, the Name above all names...

More personally, Gabriel knew that the Father was...*his* father.

A shudder of unspeakable joy went through Gabriel at Lucifer's announcement. "We are going to meet *HIM*?"

"Yes," Lucifer said, breathless as he hurried his younger friend along.

While the prospect of such an introduction was exciting beyond words, it was also terrifying. "But...but...why...what for?"

Gabriel could barely keep up with Lucifer, who seemed to have risen above him. Suddenly, he felt the rush of his guide's wings stirring the air, and when he looked down, he saw that Lucifer's feet were not touching the ground.

Neither were his own! Lucifer had lifted him with his strong hands, and his own meager wings were now aiding in the flight.

The landscape of heaven was passing beneath so quickly, he scarcely had a chance to take it in. Down the plush green of the highland on which he was born, down toward the lapping river they went. The sound of angelic music filled the rushing air, seeming to be the air itself, and not merely an ingredient of it.

Before Gabriel had a chance to ask why they were heading toward the river, Lucifer drew back and glided softly toward the bank. Gabriel tripped against the ground, nearly slamming into the more accomplished flier. Together, they had managed to land beside a huddle of three other angels, who were helping each other find their balance as they stood, for the first time, upright.

As Gabriel caught his breath, he and Lucifer watched the angelic tangle, three burly fellows in an awkward struggle to look dignified as their knees buckled beneath them.

When the three, at last, gained a measure of decorum, Lucifer stepped up to them.

"Good day, friends," he said.

Gabriel noticed their looks of amazement as they laid eyes on the brilliant being, obviously recognizing his superior majesty and aura of experience. But Gabriel was also amazed by the beauty and glory of these three who were, like himself, novices.

The trio were about equal in stature and size, each of them exquisitely handsome and strong, and endowed with the same sort of stubbly wings which Gabriel sported. They were also garbed in short tunics and mail chest-coverings, like those which Gabriel wore, but their distinct personalities were immediately apparent.

The first to reply to Lucifer's greeting was slightly taller than the other two. Hair of flaming red was his most noteworthy physical attribute, and it seemed to fit his robust, outgoing manner. Reaching forward, as he braced himself against his long sword, he managed to stop wobbling and clasped Lucifer's hand warmly.

"Good day to you, sir," he said.

Seeing the sword and the other shields and weapons upon the ground, Gabriel suddenly remembered his own armaments. In his haste to follow Lucifer, he had left them on the hillside! Chagrined, he glanced behind him, but the spot where he was born was so distant, he could not make it out from here. Swallowing hard, he turned again to the introductions and tried to focus on his new companions.

What color was his own hair? he wondered, seeing that each of these fellows seemed to have been designed from a distinct palette. The red-head announced himself as Michael. With him were a brunette named Raphael and a tow-head named Uriel. Lucifer's hair, in keeping with his strength and dominance, was gleaming black.

Michael had just introduced his friends, and was reaching out to shake Gabriel's hand, when his shield, which was propped against his legs, captured Gabriel's reflection. Ah, so there was the answer! His hair was the color of spun gold! In a flash of delight, he smiled.

"Uh, Gabriel," he said, catching himself as he shook Michael's hand. "My name is Gabriel."

The meaning of the three angels' names came to him instantaneously. Uriel, in keeping with his white-hot coloring, meant *God's Fire.* Raphael, with his soothing, more moderate appearance meant *God's Comfort.* But Michael…now here was a title that gave pause.

Who is like the Lord? was the meaning of the red-head's name. And it seemed that this was as much a statement as a question.

As all of this came to Gabriel in a flash, it did not escape him that upon Michael's introduction, Lucifer seemed to stiffen. The reaction was so subtle, so nearly imperceptible, that Gabriel immediately doubted it had happened, even though the lift of the elder angel's chin, as he gave his own name, did seem a bit overstated. "Lucifer," he announced.

Silence fell over the huddle and their eyes widened more than ever. Gabriel knew they were pondering the interpretation of the word. *Son of the Morning…Son of the Morning…*

"Friends," Lucifer continued, "I know that everything is coming to you in a great rush. You have barely become aware of your own selves, but in a very brief space you will perceive your place in a spectrum so vast, that none of us will ever comprehend it. No, never…though we spend eternity in the study."

As he spoke, his four companions' attention was drawn here and there by sights and wonders which, though never dull, would eventually become commonplace to them. The angelic choir, whose numbers filled the misty distances of heaven's rolling valleys, were only one contingent of the population which was continually bursting forth with new life. Dozens of angelic sorts were arising from the ground, discovering themselves just as Gabriel had done, learning in flashes, just as he was doing, to know what their purposes were.

Such variety was represented among them, that it seemed the Father must have spent all of eternity previous just dreaming them up. Beings of lesser stature than Gabriel and his friends, but nonetheless beautiful, wore no armor, no vests of mail or metallic leggings. These, like the choir, were robed in white, but their garbs were not so ample, less flowing. They wore short tunics, and their petite bodies and lanky limbs seemed made for speed. Gabriel would learn that these were messenger angels, whose primary purpose was to carry word back and forth between heaven and realms as yet uncreated, or already created eons before. Lovely creatures with flowing hair and feminine faces, as well as large, masculine characters with muscular arms and hefty bodies filled the ranks of the guardian angels. Though they had little in common physically, they were distinguished by their somber, caring expressions, and the need to protect and defend emanated from them.

All of this section of heaven, which they would come to know as the Valley of Life, was abuzz with life beginning, growing, filling the landscape. Such a hubbub it created, as beings large and small, two-legged and four-legged, spritely, sober, commanding, playful, came to be! Yes, there were those who walked low to the ground, on furry feet or clawed and feathered legs, who purred and flapped and squealed, barked and grunted and twittered. These, Gabriel would learn, all had their purposes, and would serve good use in their own callings.

But there was no chance to ponder all of this, before the dark-haired angel was lifting, again, from the ground, his heels and toes inches from the grassy slope. "We can chat together, later," he said. "Now, we *must* be going. The Father is initiating a new project, and it is about to be placed in our charge."

The three younger angels glanced at one another, bewildered, then turned to Gabriel, who knew no more than they. There was no time for questions, so Gabriel only shrugged. Then, with the slightest spring, and flap of his short wings, he elevated himself, as if to say, "Follow me," and they watched as he hovered a moment before taking off after Lucifer.

Gabriel was pleased to see, when he glanced over his shoulder, that Michael had managed the same feat and was trailing close behind. Uriel and Raphael, as well, had left the ground.

Together the four angels followed their leader, sweeping high above the landscape toward some unknown destination.

Below, a low range of mountains separated the first valley from a second, known as the Valley of Service, where a more experienced populace went about its occupations. Vast confluences of dells and hills, ribboned with silver streams and coursing waterfalls, were dotted with glistening villages and hamlets, where shops were being tended, parks were being pruned, schools were being taught, wagons and pedestrians moved along the roadways.

But, though all of this was new to Gabriel, it appeared that something more than routine activity was also afoot. He sensed it in the air, mingling with the music but apart from the music, itself. Everywhere along the ground angels gathered in excited conversation, hands waving, wings flapping, faces radiant.

Rushing along the roads and byways, messenger angels scurried with documents beneath their arms, heading out to spread word of some sort to far flung corners of many realms. Gabriel would later learn that there were administrative positions assigned to numberless beings who had charge of territories and empires beyond the perimeter of heaven. "Powers, principalities, dominions," they were called, both the places and the administrators, themselves.

But for now, it was enough that Gabriel realized something marvelous was transpiring.

Turning to Lucifer, he was about to question what was up and whether it related to the New Project he had spoken of, when the elder angel suddenly slowed a bit in his sleek flight, looking off toward the northern horizon with wistful eyes.

"What is it?" Gabriel asked, catching up with him.

Following Lucifer's gaze, he saw a glow of golden light in the far, far distance. Like an aurora, it seemed to throb and move with an energy more than that of mere light.

As his companions gathered around him, hovering high above the ground and studying the distant glow, Lucifer's voice was low and respectful.

"The City Celeste," he said, "whose crown is the Father's throne."

CHAPTER 3

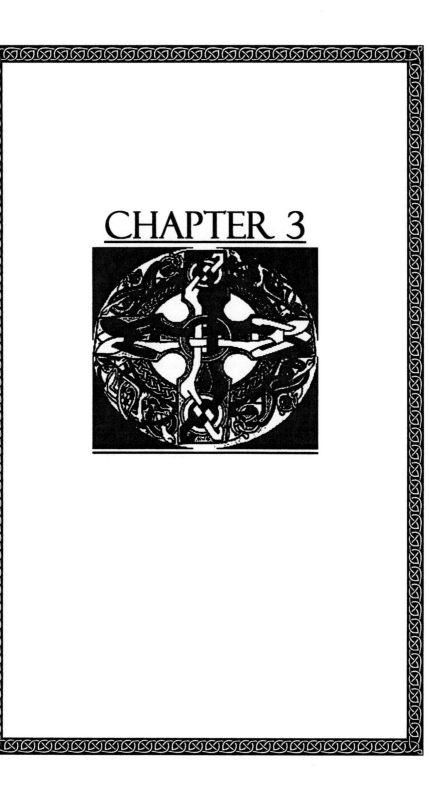

abriel could not imagine anything more beautiful than the scenery over which they traveled, the rolling hills, rushing streams, deep forests and flowered dells within the Valley of Service. If the City Celeste was more spectacular, it would surely take the breath away.

But, his mind was filled with wondering what the Father would be like, how he would look, what he would say.

He had become confident enough with his flying ability, that he dared, for one moment, to close his eyes, trying to envision God Almighty. The sweet breeze ruffled his golden hair and suddenly it seemed he heard a sweeping through the air at his back. Jolting, he looked behind him and was stunned to find that his wings had begun to grow, spreading out like feathered sails.

Wheeling about, he glanced at his companions, whose wings were, likewise, becoming large, lustrous and billowing.

In that brief interlude, the landscape had also changed dramatically, and Lucifer, at the head of the group, began rising, rising. Rolling hills had given way to cliffs and soaring peaks streaked with cascading waterfalls, so tall the tops were lost amid misty heights where brilliant shafts of light descended from some unseen source.

Suddenly, Lucifer was improvising, spinning and looping in his flight, filling the air with joyous laughter. As Gabriel and the others watched his peculiar behavior, they felt compelled to join his antics and were amazed at their new abilities, as they tested the air with loops, dives and sashays.

"What has happened to us?" Gabriel cried, racing up to Lucifer and matching his acrobatics.

Lucifer laughed aloud. "Amazing, isn't it? When we draw near to the Father, nothing is impossible!"

"I was just now trying to imagine what he is like," Gabriel said, breathless. "At that moment, my wings began to grow!"

Lucifer slowed down and said thoughtfully, "You will find that when you dwell on the Father, you are given what you need to lift you to him."

This was a profound concept, but one which would have to wait. The steeps were becoming difficult, cool downdrafts spilling over them like water. Gabriel was obliged to focus on his ascent. "Father...I am coming," he whispered, and with that he was buoyed up, up.

They were into the mists, now. But, at the same time, the shafts of light that emanated from the unseen source were becoming more intense. Suddenly, with a whoosh that preceded silence, the cool drafts ceased, the ridge of the highland gave way to broad horizon and a third, vast valley spread forth. Set directly in the center of it was a gemlike city with brilliant towers, spires, and gates of pearly white, a city so enormous there was no accounting for the size.

Gabriel and his friends settled to the ground, their feet touching down on the shore of a flawless sea, which lay like a foyer before the pearly gates. Lucifer, who had planted himself upon a glassine rock, pointed toward the metropolis like a beacon. "The City Celeste," he announced. Then, his arm sweeping across the waters, he added, "And this is called the Crystal Sea, for its waters are so pure, we can see through to the bottom."

Gabriel and the others leaned over and studied the distant floor of the sea. Aquamarine in hue, it gave the waters what color they had. "The grains of the seabed are made of sapphire stone," Lucifer explained. "Sometimes it washes ashore and you can scoop it up with your hands."

The four companions smiled at the thought, and Gabriel kicked at a patch of sapphire with his sandaled toe.

"We must be off," Lucifer said.

The angels sped toward the city, trying not to look directly into the brilliant light that shone from its crown. "What causes the shining?" Gabriel inquired.

Lucifer grew somber, and picked his words carefully. "Heaven's light is the nature of the Father, his Spirit and his Son," he said.

Gabriel picked up on the hesitation in Lucifer's voice. It seemed that the reference to the Son caught strangely in his throat. But he attributed this to the profound respect the mere mention of him provoked, a respect as fundamental as life and heartbeats and substance.

The angels, following their leader, proceeded now on foot. There would be no sashays, no loop-the-loops. A deep sense of solemnity overcame them, and they walked with their heads bowed, their fabulous wings folded humbly behind them.

They skirted the Crystal Sea and approached the great gates. Because there was nothing upon the expansive seashore with which to compare them, they were much further away than they had appeared, and it took a good long time to reach them.

The gates, when they attained them, soared over their heads to the height of many stories. Gleaming white, they seemed to ripple with an internal luster that added a thousand soft hues to the sheen, and inset between the posts and pediments of each gate were bands of translucent gold, wide as an angel's hand. Positioned to either side of the entrance were sentries who were twice the height of the visitors. Gabriel's throat went dry at the sight of these awesome creatures. Dressed in mail from head to toe, they brandished gleaming swords that flashed light of many colors.

"Who goes there?" one of them cried, as they drew within sight.

Lucifer showed no trepidation. Throwing his shoulders back, he called loudly, "Lucifer, Son of the Morning, and my comrades!"

The sentries stiffened and clicked their heels together the instant he called out his name. It seemed they recognized it, and though they were twice his size, they stepped aside, bowing their heads.

"We have been awaiting your arrival, Master Lucifer," they said. "Please, enter."

Gabriel felt the hair on his arms rise in gooseflesh. Michael and the others glanced his way, as though he might understand what was transpiring. But, he could only shrug and fall in behind their mysterious leader.

Whoever Lucifer was, he was of such importance that the gates of the eternal city opened at his very approach. Gabriel did not know whether to love him or fear him.

CHAPTER 4

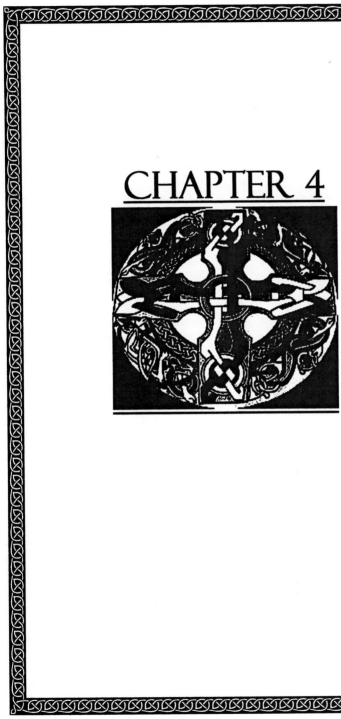

f the second valley through which they had traveled, the Valley of Service, had seemed busy with unexplained excitement, the streets and greens of the crystalline plateau, the City Celeste, were even more so. Here the population was not only as active, but was at least as varied, as those outside, and many of the beings who inhabited Celeste were of the same sorts who lived in the lower region. In fact, Gabriel would learn, all heavenly beings came and went between the second valley and the celestial plateau on a regular basis.

The throne room, which most creatures rarely entered, was the innermost court of heaven, the inner chamber of the Mountain of the Lord, and the abode of God himself. The fact that Gabriel and his friends had been summoned to appear there, spoke volumes about the intentions God had for them. In fact, it would only be eons afterward, when he would experience existence on a much lower plane, that Gabriel would begin to comprehend something of the great honor that had devolved to him when the Creator had made him.

As they passed over the bridge leading from the gates to the city square, they found clusters of angels in animated conversation, some giving orders to others who hurried off as though in compliance with instructions. The arrival of Lucifer and his little band did not go unnoticed, however: as they passed through the streets, angels stepped aside with the same awe-filled expressions and unexplained deference shown by the gatekeepers.

As for the streets, themselves, they were noteworthy for their fabulous beauty. The pavement appeared to be made from the same gold which had formed the bars on the pearly gates, so pure as to be almost transparent. When Gabriel looked down, he saw his reflection in the lucent surface, his entire being reproduced in gilded tones, and his yellow hair having the appearance of spun platinum.

Lining the streets were buildings of fabulous construction, decked with finely wrought archways and latticed terraces and lined with courts filled with all manner of budding trees, singing birds and bubbling fountains. Through the open windows could be glimpsed the homely activities of the residents, as they ate at sumptuously laden tables and chatted amiably together. Every abode was a mansion, each with its own distinctive style and ambiance, some more formal, more delicate, than others, some rustic with bronze and coarse wooden fittings, the styles as varied as the personalities of the inhabitants.

As they passed over the bridge... they found clusters of angels in animated conversation, some giving orders to others...

The streets were a hubbub of joyous activity, and permeating everything, surrounding it and embodying it, was something like a song, a praise, which seemed to literally grow out of the activities of the citizens. "Holy... holy... holy..." it whispered, a sound and yet more than a sound. It was a subtle throbbing of life, undergirding and representing all that went on in this happy place. "Holy ... holy ... holy ... Lord God Almighty ... which wert and art and evermore shalt be..."

Yet, there was also a pervasive sense of leisure here, all work an evident joy, and no stress or strain accompanied what was done, but only song and mirth. Gabriel would come to learn that this was called the Valley of Worship.

Broad parklands broke up the metropolitan scene, the homes of the citizens set against foregrounds and backgrounds of green, elysian botany, where streams and ponds laced through the landscape and deep causeways were graced with the unfurled sails of private vessels.

The aromas of a thousand flowering plant species tickled Gabriel's nose and the smells from a hundred kitchens made him salivate. He had never eaten. Food was something he had yet to experience. But, he was learning the feel of hunger.

Lucifer glanced over his shoulder and gave a wink. "Just wait 'til you see the food in the throne room!" he said. "It is worth the journey just to enjoy that."

"Food?" Michael said, catching up with them. "The Father eats?"

"Of course," Lucifer said. "He does not do so because he must, but because it is part of the enjoyment of life. He, after all, created food and our liking for it."

Michael's stomach growled, and his four companions laughed.

The golden streets were becoming steeper, now, passing through thick forestland. Suddenly, as though leaping to life, an enormous castle sprang into view. Surely they had come upon it by the natural incline of their journey, but it seemed to appear out of nowhere, and the four younger angels stopped still in their tracks.

Lucifer stopped with them, and nodded in understanding. "So," he said, taking a deep breath. "Here we have it...the highest of the heavenlies, the Mountain of the Lord, and the home of God himself."

As though set on a spiral staircase, so high and steep that its pinnacles were visible only through moving clouds, the gigantic structure gleamed and glistened. The brilliance which permeated all of heaven had obviously emanated from this point, and the castle was, itself, athrob with light. Almost it seemed to be made of light, yet, as they allowed their eyes to gaze upon it, they became accustomed to the radiance. To look away was unthinkable.

Instead, it drew them on, beckoning to them with an internal music, a sound as much a part of it as the light.

Now, barely thinking about it, they found themselves ascending, approaching the lowest rung of the radiant stairway. As they drew near and began their ascent toward the castle proper, they saw that what had appeared from a distance to be the borders of the stairs were, in fact, lines of angels, all aglow and singing, thousands upon thousands of them.

"Holy, holy, holy is the Lord," they chorused, "God and Father of us all."

Gabriel's heart was flooded with joy at the sound. *Yes...he is my Father, as well,* he thought. *And I am about to meet him!*

What a wondrous congregation they were, beautiful, handsome, strong. Through the glow of their beings, he made out both masculine and feminine persons, tall, short, strong, delicate, winged, armored, robed, tuniced, all in garbs befitting various callings. As he and his friends passed up the stairway, many reached out to greet them, their touch warm and reassuring.

Gabriel felt, in that moment, that he had come home. He felt as though, until now, he had only been born, but not truly lived.

Yet, what did he know of life, or of anything? He had existed such a short while.

As for Lucifer, he had apparently been around much longer. He had already met the Father. Perhaps, once one met the Father, all things became clear, all questions vanished.

In a moment, he would know.

Lucifer had reached the top step, and all of them gathered on the ivory platform that led to the inner Hall of Light.

"The throne room," Lucifer whispered, leaning close to his followers. "Be very still, now."

He need not have told them to do this. They could not have spoken for their dry throats. Keeping their wings close to their bodies, they huddled together, following their leader in unison step, their arms intertwined together

Nor did they look up, but kept their eyes to the ivory floor, until they came upon two gigantic seraphim who blocked the final doorway with enormous, silver wings.

Gabriel shuddered when his escort gave his name, once again, as though it were a passport. "Lucifer, Son of the Morning."

There was the briefest of pauses, as the two seraphim bowed their heads and looked almost as if they would fall before him. Lucifer gave them the oddest of looks, and suddenly they lurched upright.

With a whoosh of their great silvery wings, the doorway was revealed, and the newcomers were obliged to step forth, into the presence of God.

CHAPTER 5

he brilliance of the inner court might have been too much to bear, except that within seconds of their entrance, the angels acclimated to it. What was initially a glaring white quickly distilled into colors and hues that made the furnishings and other entities of the chamber distinguishable. Within moments, their eyes adjusted and their squinting became wide-eyed wonder.

Since their gaze was, at first, turned toward the floor, as they entered with heads bowed in fearful reverence, the first thing to become apparent to them was a broad runner of carpet, soft to the feet, its design of the most amazing intricacy. Royal purples and cobalt blues made up the background, with golden patterns of wings and globes and shining orbs laid against it. The symbols meant little to them, now, but would come to stand for much that the future held.

They did not look to either side of them, but sensed, without turning their heads, that there were many persons in the chamber, all in an attitude of reverent service. As their eyes grew accustomed to the light and to the shapes and colors it revealed, so did their other senses quickly register a medley of impressions: a soft, pervasive sound of music; a rich and soothing fragrance; and an all encompassing, comforting warmth.

The music, which was more like a rhythmic chant than a full-blown chorus, arose from courts adjacent to the throne room, on either side. It swelled like a gentle tide, repeating itself over and over, yet without creating any trancelike mood. Somehow, the words, though stated again and again, were always fresh.

"Holy... holy... holy... Lord God Almighty ... which wert, and art and evermore shalt be..."

Mingled with these repeated phrases were others, each distinctive, each personal to the speaker. In a multitude of voices they were spoken, each statement apparently from the heart of some unseen worshipper, and rendered as though for the first time:

"Glory to God, the Almighty, the King of Creation...Oh, my soul praise him, for he is love's manifestation."

"All ye who hear...now to his temple draw near! Join me in glad adoration!"

Yet, though the songs swelled with feeling, they were almost a whisper, breeze-like in their tenderness.

The singers were, like the doorkeepers, called seraphim. There were thousands of them, and their vast courts spread beyond the inner chamber for many leagues.

Wound between the words, as though part of them, were fragrances, sweet beyond expression. The aromas arose from the songs themselves, on the breath of the singers, and wafted through the open archways and windows of the inner chamber.

Gabriel dared to lift his eyes just enough to see that the pervasive warmth of the throne room was due to heat emanating from an enormous, circular altar in the center of the floor. Made entirely of bronze, the radiant altar was heaped with glowing coals, beside which sat a pair of gigantic silver tongs.

Suddenly, a voice boomed behind the visitors. "Go forward!" it commanded.

Gabriel did not stop to analyze the source of the voice, which was even more intimidating than the sentinels who had scrutinized them at the head of the staircase. Lurching, he and his companions did as they were told, following the broad blue carpet toward the brazen altar.

Before they reached it, the angel with the booming voice passed over their heads and landed between them and the fire. Holding up his hand, he commanded them to stop.

"Release your weapons, lower your shields!" he ordered.

Gabriel, having left his armor in the first valley, watched as the other three novices placed their gear upon the floor. Immediately, it was gathered up by attendants and whisked away.

Then, in one slick movement, the intercepting angel lifted the silver tongs from off the altar, grabbed a hot coal and flashed it before them.

"Lift up your heads!" he commanded.

To disobey was beyond thought. In unison, the visitors did as they were told, and the mighty one brought the glowing coal before them, touching it to their lips one by one, before they had time to resist.

Though Gabriel had never experienced pain, he anticipated it as the coal lit upon his open mouth. But, there was no pain, only a jolt of awe that made his knees buckle.

Suddenly, he crumpled to the floor, side by side with his friends, whose strength had failed them as well. Completely overcome, they knelt for a good long while, as the angel with the tongs hovered overhead, examining them.

Then, with a whoosh, he was off, and they were left in the middle of the floor, as countless eyes looked on.

It occurred to Gabriel that the music had now tapered down, so soft that it was barely audible, the fragrance of the chamber seemed to dissipate to a vapor and the warmth of the fire cooled a bit.

All was still, motionless, as though in expectation.

Then, from beyond the fire, there was movement. Gabriel felt strength returning to his body, and with a little effort he lifted his head. Apparently his friends felt the same impulse, for as he looked toward them, he saw that they were looking at him. One by one, they turned their gaze toward the throne, now visible beyond the point where the glare of the flashing coals had waned.

"Come forward, children," a voice beckoned.

They knew it on the instant, recognized it like the pulse of their own hearts. The Father had spoken!

Infused with strength, they rose and circled past the fire, two to one side and three to the other. Gabriel stood, trembling, beside Lucifer and Michael; Uriel and Raphael quaked together. Lined up before the throne, they raised their eyes and took in their first sight of God.

To their profound amazement, he appeared to be much like themselves. Strong, beautiful, only so much more so that there were no limits to the descriptors. His hair was pure white, but he looked ageless. His eyes were kind and all-knowing. His snowy beard, plaited with streaks of brilliant silver, cascaded to his lap, where his huge hands held a golden scepter, through which a constant whirr of lights pulsated. His skin was iridescent, nearly translucent, and of no color whatever, yet he was utterly solid, as though spirit and light had bonded together to form the substance of time and thought.

"Yes, yes, come on, now," he urged them. "Don't be afraid, will you?"

Gabriel sensed delight in the Father's tone, a bit of humor, even. "We have much to do, you know."

No, he didn't know. Yet, somehow, he realized that he was needed.

It was not apparent, at first, that others sat with the Father. The newcomers heard him say a few things that sounded conversational, but they thought he only spoke to himself.

"We have done well," they heard him say. "Some of our best work, yet!"

At last, however, they could distinguish two other entities beside him, one seated on his right, and the other leaning over the back of the throne, in intimate closeness.

"Yes," they were agreeing. "These will do. These will do."

Now the chamber flooded back to life. The music of the outer courts rose again, and the fragrance filled the air. The coals of the fire glowed fresh, and there was a bustle about the room, as though some sort of preparations were underway.

As this transpired, the Father leaned down and greeted Lucifer warmly.

"Son of the Morning," he said with a smile. "You have done well."

Lucifer was not so self-possessed this time. To Gabriel's relief, he seemed to effuse genuine humility, bowing his great, dark head, and clicking his heels together.

"It was nothing, Master," he said. "Their nobility and glory was obvious. I am sure they will all do their best for you."

At this, the Father leaned back and communed with the two beside him. Then, once more, he sat forward.

"Gabriel, Michael, Uriel and Raphael," he said, each name a smile on his lips, "we have no wish to keep you in suspense. You have been called here for a great purpose. But, you must be weary and hungry after your long journey."

Clapping his hands, he bade them turn around. Between themselves and the altar of coals a small table had been spread, with goblets of wine and plates of sweet, white cake.

"Take, eat," he said to them. "And with each bite you take, your eyes will begin to be opened to your purpose."

Tentatively, the four angels stepped to the altar. Lucifer, glancing at the Father, understood that he was, also, to partake.

As Gabriel took his first bite of food, it was an experience he would remember always. Not only was this his first knowledge of taste and culinary delight, but suddenly, as he partook, his soul swelled with eagerness, a mysterious sense of anticipation.

CHAPTER 6

abriel and his companions sat on low, upholstered stools at the alabaster table in the Father's throne room. The servants of the chamber waited on them attentively, filling their cups and replenishing their plates with the strange white cake, until they could not have eaten another bite.

Sweet and gratifying, the cake seemed to be more than mere food, enlivening their minds and charging their hearts with expectation. Even Lucifer seemed unfamiliar with its effects, and for once, he and his four comrades were on even ground.

At length, the Father addressed them.

"I know that all of you are wondering why you have been summoned."

Gabriel and his friends watched as the Almighty rose from his throne and stepped down to the ivory floor. Behind him, now clearly visible, was the one who sat on a throne to his right. He had been there all along, to be sure, but had been nearly indistinguishable from the Father. Just as Lucifer had said would happen, the instant Gabriel laid eyes on this person, he knew who he was.

The Son!

It was only a thought, but it shouted itself into his very core. Yes, surely, this was the Son, whom Lucifer had spoken of with such reverence. And Gabriel knew that anyone who could inspire awe in Lucifer must be amazing, indeed.

But, the Father was speaking again, and Gabriel tore his eyes away from the Son.

"You have surely sensed the excitement in the air, as you crossed the valleys and mountains to come here," the Father was saying. "Perhaps you have heard that there are great plans afoot?"

The four younger angels nodded enthusiastically. "They could not help but notice," Lucifer replied. "I told my friends, here, that some wondrous work was about to unfold, though I, of course, knew little more than they."

The last few words bore the vaguest hint of dejection, as though Lucifer felt he should be privy to more than he was.

The Father observed him lovingly. "And did you tell them that I shall be needing their assistance, and *yours*, Son of the Morning?"

Lucifer perked up a bit. "I did, Master," he said with a nod, "though I believe they would have known it in their hearts, well enough."

The Lord seemed happy to hear this and began to walk back and forth, as though deep in thought. "Where to begin?" he said.

Turning about, he pointed toward a wide archway that gave a view of the entire valley below, the city through which they had traveled and the steeps they had climbed. Suddenly, with a flash of his scepter, the scene changed, and the angels' hearts leapt to their throats.

All that had been visible was suddenly overwashed with pure blackness, a swimming cauldron of darkness and emptiness. It was as if nothing existed, outside this chamber.

The servants who lined the walls gasped and everyone, except the two beside the great throne, was filled with dread.

The Father studied their fear filled faces. "Have you ever wondered what things would be like, had I never existed?" he asked. "Have you ever wondered what would be, if there were no First Cause?"

Of course, they had not wondered. For all those present, existence was a given, a reality with no beginning, except their first awareness of it. Ultimate beginnings and endings were not in their frame of reference.

But, here was a question being put to them plainly, and it required a stretch beyond all comprehension for them to even entertain it.

"Ah, I see," the Father said. "I should not have expected you might imagine any such thing."

Again, he flashed his scepter and the valleys, mountains, city, all returned as it had been. A sigh went up from the onlookers, but they had been shaken to their souls, and would never be quite the same thereafter.

The Father returned to his throne and sat silent for a long while. For once, the music outside had come to a full stop, all was quiet, all heaven tingled with wonder.

"Children, I do not show you this to frighten you. You have been created in light and are beings of light. You have known nothing but my love from your first breath. And you serve me without any thought to the contrary."

Gabriel sat on the edge of his stool, his eyes riveted on the Father, whose every word was precious as his own heart beating.

"But, what if it were not so?" the Father went on. "What if things were not so clear? Obedience not so natural? What if..."

He stopped, a shudder going through his own divine being. "What if somewhere, in some way, the light ceased to shine, or never shone in the first place? What if light were to come upon a place as though never before existing, and what if the darkness fought to overcome it?"

The five angels, even Lucifer, were rapt. Gabriel's skin tingled, and despite the Father's injunction, he could not help but be afraid. Sitting up straight, he dared to raise a hand, hoping to be seen.

The Father spotted his gesture immediately, and a thrill went through Gabriel as he heard his name spoken by God Almighty for the second time.

"Gabriel," the Father addressed him, "you have a question?"

"I do, My Lord," he said, slipping off the stool and falling to his knees. "I...I..."

"Yes, son, speak," the Father said kindly.

"I do not understand. What, exactly, is...darkness?"

The Father glanced toward the archway where He had invoked the black scene only moments before.

"Uh, yes, I know what it looks like, Father," Gabriel said, "but, I do not understand what it is. I have seen shadows in the highlands and deep purples in the river. But, this darkness seems so much more..."

He was at a loss for words.

" 'Dark' ?" the Father filled in.

Gabriel felt foolish.

The Father gave a sober smile. "The sort of darkness I am referring to is the utter absence of light, the opposite of life, the absence of good, a veil hiding my own face. Can you grasp this?"

Gabriel rolled his eyes toward Michael, who was dumbstruck.

"It is a place in which truth is unknowable, and error is natural...where obedience is not the norm, for those who walk in darkness cannot perceive good and evil, having no knowledge of either."

Gabriel trembled. "What an unhappy place that would be!" he groaned.

Michael was perplexed, his brow furrowed. "Is there such a place, Father?" he asked. Then, clenching his fist, he pounded his knee. "If there is, we must go there, to correct this great wrong!"

The Father smiled at Michael's boldness, then rose once again and walked past the brazen altar, where he stood upon the broad, blue runner. Glancing about the room, catching each eye in a fleeting moment of fathomless contact, he gave the most stunning pronouncement he had ever made.

"I am about to conduct an experiment," He said. "Not even I shall decide the outcome."

The audience was mesmerized, and a low huzza filled the chamber. "What did he say?" some asked, incredulous. As his statement was repeated, again and again, passing from the chamber to the outer courts, going from angel to angel, to the seraphim and their great chorus, to the lesser angels and even to the four-footed beasts who played in forest and field, it seemed all of heaven would shortly be filled with it.

Not even I...not even I... shall decide the outcome...outcome...outcome...

It echoed through the highlands, past the Crystal Sea, through the valleys, through the towns, down, down, to the very border of the green knoll where Gabriel had been born.

The five angels poised on their stools, Lucifer tense as a cat, Michael clenching and unclenching his fists, Gabriel dumbfounded.

And the Father spoke again.

"I shall create darkness, and I shall split it with light. I shall create beings who can exist in either atmosphere. And I shall give them *choice*."

This last word rang strangely in the ears of all the listeners.

Choice?

Surely God's creatures made choices every day, on rudimentary levels. But it seemed that the choice God referred to was much more profound.

Brave Gabriel caught the Lord's eye, and once again, raised a hand.

But the Father knew his question, without the framing of it. He knew it rang through the hearts of all present.

"*What is this choice?* you are wondering."

Gabriel swallowed hard and sat back, lowering his head. "Yes, Sir," he whispered.

As the Father had addressed him, the word of the moment had passed through the chamber, to the outer court, down the mountainside, across the sea, through the towns, through the valleys.

Choice...choice...choice...

What WAS this choice?

The Father sat down upon his throne again, gazing out across the timeless landscape beyond his window.

"This choice," he replied, "is the option to love or not to love...me."

Nobody in the chamber had ever seen the look that imprinted itself upon the Lord's face with that statement. It was a look of wistful sadness, of fleeting...was it *regret*? Surely, God could not regret anything! Yet, he seemed unwaveringly determined, utterly bent on playing out this "experiment."

And what of the impact of these words on the hearers? Within moments, such a commotion spread through heaven that the very ground shook, the mountains quaked.

Not to love the Father? Why, this was beyond the most unthinkable of notions! The very speaking of it could have thrown everything off balance, brought snowy heights tumbling to valley bottoms, ripped the wings off angels, dissipated the sea into a froth of roiling steam...had the Father not held up his mighty hand and calmed everything.

As the great quake had passed through the chamber, it had inflicted disarray, tossing the angels to the floor. As things steadied, Gabriel managed to find his strength and pulled himself up to sit on his stool.

He looked to Lucifer for reassurance, but, much to his dismay, he found a look of grave concern upon his mentor's face.

"Master," croaked Son of the Morning, "this *choice* of which you speak…upon whom will it be tested?"

The Father did not look at Lucifer as he replied, his thoughts apparently very far away. "A new creation," he said, "a creation born out of darkness, a creation which, if it chooses to love me, will do so at the greatest of costs."

CHAPTER 7

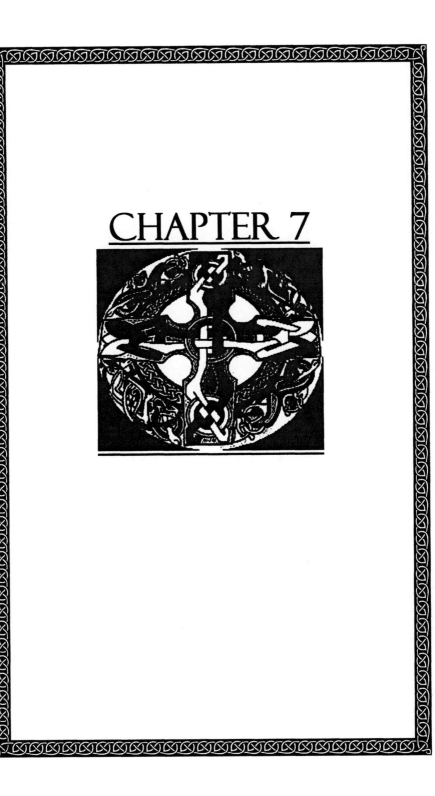

s Gabriel and his companions left the hallowed halls of the throne room, their minds were a swirl of impressions, insights, bewilderments, too numerous to sort out. Their dismissal from the chamber had been courteous and lavish, as they were each called forward to receive a touch from the Father, a gentle laying on of hands, as if they were being commissioned.

With this honor, he bestowed upon the four younger ones the designation "archangels," denoting that they were of a higher caste than most other angels, though their full purpose was not yet revealed.

They retreated down the broad stairway, celebrated on every side as though their little processional were a victory march, by the same beings who had greeted their arrival.

But no one explained to them what they were to do next.

After they had passed through the City Celeste, they breathed a little easier.

"Well, what should we make of all that?" Michael dared to ask.

Gabriel gulped and turned to Raphael and Uriel, who were so deep in thought they could not speak. Then, he glanced at Lucifer.

While all the others seemed absorbed in profound contemplation, their heads stooped and their walk tentative, Son of the Morning exhibited fresh energy. He strode down the highway with head held high, shoulders back, tread confident. For the hundredth time Gabriel wondered what he was about.

"I, for one, am going to pick out a mansion!" Lucifer announced. "Did you see that they were being constructed all along the knolls overlooking the river, in the middle valley? If we hurry, we can have our choice!"

There was that word again...*choice.* Gabriel felt a chill at the sound.

Yet, he marveled at his reaction. There was nothing wrong with choice, *per se*, not in regard to things like houses and clothing and that sort of thing. But, from now on, the word would always remind him of the Father's sad eyes, and the wistful gaze that portended things more significant.

Especially it did so, just now, when Lucifer spoke it. His pronouncement seemed brash and shallow, in light of all they had just been through.

"A mansion?" Gabriel sputtered, hurrying to keep pace with him. "How can you think of such a thing at this time?"

Michael, having the same thought, had stopped dead in his tracks, his hands on his hips.

"Shouldn't we be thinking of what the Father wants?" the red-haired angel called out. "I can't imagine that mansions are particularly important at this moment!"

Now that got a reaction from Lucifer. Stunned by Michael's audacity, he wheeled about with a scowl.

"I think a mansion is just what I need!" he replied. "Until we know precisely what the Father has in mind for us, we may as well be busy preparing for it. As for me, I intend my mansion to be a headquarters!"

What was it, lately, about words? Gabriel was hearing too many important words for the first time. Some, like *choice*, had a depth that required explanation. Others, like *headquarters*, needed none.

Michael apparently picked up on the implication instantly. "*Headquarters?*" he barked. "That's a very important announcement, Lucifer. Do you mean to set yourself up as our commander?"

Gabriel tensed. He would not have been so forthright. Something more diplomatic would have done better, he thought. Something like, "That's an interesting idea, Lucifer. Just what use did you intend for your *headquarters*?"

It was clear that Michael had a confrontational nature. Though he had never seen armies or warfare, it seemed natural for him to think in terms of commanders, followers, and such.

Whatever, the verbal gauntlet had been thrown down. Lucifer did not hesitate to pick it up.

When he did so, however, it was with a cunning that Michael had not exhibited. Facing his challenger, he was at first rigid, his chin lifted in defiance. But, quickly this attitude changed to tutorial condescension.

"I misspoke, my friend," he said suavely. "I should have been more sensitive. I presumed that all of you (he swept his hand through the air) would have considered yourselves commanders, that all of you would be eager to establish an enclave for our administration."

At this he saluted Michael, the latest new word, *administration*, hanging mysteriously between them.

Administration...

Gabriel rather liked the sound of it. It was diplomatic, to be sure, and full of heady responsibility. He figured that, after all, the Father *had* implied the five of them would be involved in some sort of *administration*.

Michael shuffled awkwardly. "V-very well..." he stammered. "If that's what you meant."

Lucifer stepped toward his downcast comrade and placed a solicitous hand on his shoulder. "We have all been through a lot," he soothed. "Our nerves are on edge. Come, let's be going."

Raphael and Uriel drew close to Michael, as Lucifer turned away. An indefinable chill had settled over them all.

Yet, Gabriel reasoned against it. Surely, Lucifer meant no harm. It was just his zealousness that made him overbearing.

As Michael and his two companions came along behind, Gabriel rushed forward to join his mentor, his heart full of turmoil.

"What is it?" the darker angel asked, seeing his young friend's pondering expression. "Have I offended you, as well?"

"Oh, no, Sir," Gabriel rasped. "Not really. You have every right to consider yourself our leader. Michael is a great one for equality, that's all."

Lucifer smirked. "I sincerely doubt equality is the issue. Someone named *Who is like the Lord?* can hardly have equality at heart."

Gabriel could scarcely believe his ears. Lucifer seemed envious!

Then, with the uncanny swiftness that repeatedly made Gabriel question his own assumptions, Lucifer took on a soft, pliant aspect.

"As for me," he said, "I really do not think of myself as anyone's *leader*." He looked faraway, as though pricked to the heart by the very suggestion. "It is only that I have been here longer than all of you. I am *Son of the Morning*. If The Father means for me to head up the dawn of his New Creation, how can I refuse?"

CHAPTER 8

ichael, Uriel, Raphael and Gabriel sat in the cool shadows of a streamside garden. Over the hill toward a new housing development, the sounds of building and industry filled the air.

It was an active time in the history of heaven. The Father's creative nature had always imbued the realm with joyous work, but lately the citizens of the heavenlies had been spurred to ever greater achievements in art, architecture and invention. One of the main activities was the creation of fabulous homes for the ever-increasing population.

Of all things God enjoyed making, beings of breath were his favorites. There was apparently no end to his imagination, when it came to the endowing of his realm with wonderful life forms. The more magnificent of these creatures, the angels and archangels, the seraphim and cherubim and a multitude of other angelic castes, required housing, not for protection (for there was no danger here) but for the joy of privacy, solitude and the fostering of individuality.

The four comrades listened to the sounds of carpentry and masonry from the far side of the hill, and wondered what Lucifer might be finding in his quest for the perfect "headquarters."

It was evident that Michael still bristled from the upbraiding he had received. His friends sat beside him in silence.

Gabriel's heart hurt. He did not have much experience to draw on, but he sensed that something was dreadfully wrong, that heaven was not meant for unhappiness, and that this contention between Michael and Lucifer was the first black spot ever to cloud a pristine horizon.

He wondered if the Father knew about it, and what he would say if he did.

True to his name, *God's Comfort*, Raphael sat closest to Michael, providing encouragement by his mere presence. Uriel, *God's Fire*, seemed to pulsate purity, a desire to avenge his friend and wipe the slate clean once and for all.

"I do believe that Lucifer thinks the Father has put him in charge of this New Creation," Uriel said.

Raphael's brow knit and he rested his chin in his hands.

Michael, slump shouldered, shook his head.

Gabriel took a breath, about to speak, when the others stopped him with a look. "Now, Gabriel," Uriel started, "don't go defending Lucifer. We know he is your mentor. He is ours, as well. But, even you must admit there is something … strange … about him."

Gabriel looked away, feeling unjustly

judged. "I wasn't going to defend him," he objected. "I was going to say that he was around before our time."

Michael could not disagree. "Very well, then. Do you think Lucifer is in charge?"

Gabriel hesitated. "If the Father has said so, yes. But, in the long run, I don't think any of us, Lucifer or you or me, or any of us, will be in charge."

Raphael's interest was piqued. "It sounds as though you have some idea of who the leader will be."

Gabriel was at a loss. "No, I can't say that I do," he admitted.

They were all surprised when Raphael pursued his own question. "Well," he began, "I have been giving it a lot of thought. And..."

The other three leaned in close, as though a great secret were about to be revealed.

"...and," they prodded him.

Raphael got a faraway look. "Remember when we were in the Father's court? Remember the one who sat beside him?"

Michael and Uriel acted as though a light had gone on in their heads. "Of course!" Michael exclaimed. "Who was he?"

"I do not know," Raphael replied. "But there was something about him ... something far more glorious than all of Lucifer's glory."

Gabriel swallowed, his throat dry. "I ... I know who he is," he said.

The three turned wondering eyes on him. "Tell us, then!" Uriel demanded.

"He is called simply *the Son*."

The three looked dubious. "No, really," Gabriel insisted. "That is one of the first things Lucifer ever told me. He also told me that I would know him when I saw him. And, I did. So did you, though you did not know his name."

The three knew that Gabriel referred to a strange, overwhelming feeling of awe which they had each experienced when the Son's presence dawned on them.

Michael's voice was surprisingly small when he said, "But, such a strange name. Doesn't one of his magnificence deserve a mightier name than that?"

Uriel agreed. "Yes. After all, we are all sons of God. Surely he is worthy of a greater name than that."

Gabriel shrugged. "I suppose it is a matter of emphasis," he suggested. "Perhaps in its simplicity lies the power of the name. For he is not just one son among many, but THE Son."

Raphael pondered this. "It seems that no word or name can be taken lightly in this realm. Every syllable is full of portent."

Uriel nodded. "So, what do you make of the

THE Son's name. Why is he THE Son, and not just one of many?"

Gabriel straightened. "I have given this some thought, as well," he said. "I believe it all ties in with Raphael's intuition that the Son will be the leader of the New Creation."

"Do tell…go on then," Michael prodded.

"Well, if he is THE Son, he must not be a created being, but the very expression of the Father, the essence, the emanating thought. And if he is all of this, nothing can be created without him."

Michael was amazed. "I didn't know you were a philosopher as well as a hero!" he said with a laugh.

Gabriel, *God's Hero*, blushed. "So far, I have not proven any heroism."

Raphael felt a shudder cross his shoulders. "I think it will not be long before you have ample opportunity. If my hunch is right, Lucifer is not going to stand still to see the coveted leadership go to the Son."

Once again, Gabriel found himself resisting any such thought. "I don't believe it is right to judge him so quickly!" he cried. "Lucifer is a beautiful being, the most glorious of all God's angels. Why, he was the one who first told me about the Son. Why would he do that, if he is his rival?"

He had them there. All of them were silent, until Raphael sadly said, "Perhaps he loves the Son. Who could not? But, perhaps he does not know himself so well as he should."

CHAPTER 9

ven as they huddled together, contemplating Raphael's words, a shadow deeper than that of the grove fell over them, sending a chill to their hearts. They knew that Lucifer had returned and stood watching them from behind, blocking the light that perpetually streamed from the distant mountain of God.

When they looked up, however, they were greeted by the dazzling smile which Lucifer so often donned, a smile that seemed, in itself, to contain all the light of heaven.

"Why the gloomy faces, comrades?" he called out. Then, lifting a hand, he bade them get to their feet and follow him. "I want your counsel regarding the place I have chosen."

The four archangels looked sideways at one another. "Very well," Gabriel replied. "We are coming."

Michael shrugged and Raphael sighed. Uriel begrudgingly stood up, and they all complied.

Lucifer had already started back, and they hastened to catch up, as he expostulated on the attributes of the mansion he had chosen. "It is modest," he said. "I don't think we should be ostentatious. As our responsibilities grow, so will the grandeur expected of us. But, it is lovely. I think you will agree."

On and on he went, telling the number of rooms, the vistas from the balconies, and so on, as they nearly ran to keep up with him. Gabriel fairly expected Lucifer to take off flying, so enraptured was he in his find.

Over several hills they traveled, past many mansions in various stages of construction. Countless muscular angels in short tunics, their legs protected by bindings and their hands by heavy gloves, hoisted girders into place, hauled barrows full of bricks, stone and mortar, and wielded hammers on the framework of complex buildings.

In a place like heaven, no work was really necessary. The Father could have seen to it that buildings appeared instantaneously, with no effort at all. But, the joy the builder angels took in their labors belied such an arrangement. The Father knew his creatures needed to share in his creativity, and so achievement was the motivator of the heavenly economy.

At last they came to the highest of the knolls round about. On its summit sat a colossal palace, embellished with spires and turrets, all of gleaming bronze.

"*Modest?*" Raphael said. "Did you say the place was *modest?*"

Lucifer gritted his teeth, and smiled again.

"Compared to what it shall eventually be, yes," he replied.

Swooping ahead of them, his feet leaving the ground, Lucifer headed for the front portico of the grand domicile. Gabriel could sense his friends' eyes on him, asking if he did not see just how self-absorbed Lucifer was. He avoided their gazes and followed his mentor, the others bringing up the rear.

With extravagant gestures, Lucifer led them from room to room, showing off his fabulous choice. "Here we shall set up our map room, where we can plot and watch the development of the New Creation. There we shall meet with the heads of the committees, who will carry out our plans."

He took them up a wide, winding staircase, and showed them where their own apartments would be, complete with lounges, fountains, gardens and verandas that took in sweeping views.

At last, he bade them sit in a sumptuous parlor, already furnished with deep, soft settees and fabulous carpets.

"Well," he said with a dramatic sigh, "what do you think?"

Michael had had it with Lucifer's grandiosity. He was so angry, he was no longer intimidated by Son of the Morning.

"Why don't you just take over the throne room of the Almighty?" he snarled. "Surely nothing is too good for you, Lucifer!"

To the utter amazement of Gabriel and the others, Lucifer bristled for only a fleeting second. Instead, he appeared to be wounded to the core.

"Why, Michael, how can you speak so?" he said. "I have only done what I think is right for the work ahead. After all, it is not for myself, alone, that I have chosen this place. We will all share in this together."

Michael drew back and shook his head. "I cannot speak for my friends, here," he said, "but I want no part of this folly!"

There is was, again, another new word. *Folly!* Such a potent sound! Though Michael, himself, had never heard nor spoken the word before, it sprang to his lips full-blown from the well-spring of eternal wisdom, with no need for definition.

Gabriel, Uriel and Raphael cringed, fearing an altercation then and there.

But, there was no chance for the contest to play itself out. What Lucifer might have done, how he might have reacted, no one would know just now, for, as things turned out, the drama was interrupted.

Footsteps in the hall beyond the parlor drew their attention to the doorway. Two bright, shining angels stood there, and the archangels recognized them as envoys from the Father's throne room.

"Master Lucifer," they said, clicking their heels together in salute, "we bring word from the inner sanctum."

Lucifer stood to his feet, shaking off the heat of recent moments. "Greetings, sirs," he replied. "I am at my Lord's service."

The messengers bowed their heads, as one of them announced, "You are being summoned to meet with His Majesty the Son, Prince of Heaven, by the Tree of Life."

Lucifer seemed taken aback, his face slightly twitching.

"It is my honor," he rasped, clicking his own heels and bowing to them.

"We have brought a chariot to courier you," the second envoy said. "Come with us."

Lucifer lifted his chin and did not grace his companions with so much as a glance, as he followed the messengers out the door.

Michael, Gabriel, Raphael and Uriel watched his departure inquisitively, wondering what the Son could want with someone like him.

But, they were not to be left without answers. Just as the envoys departed with their charge, one of them turned back and leaned in the doorway, motioning to them. "You are welcome to come, as well," he said. "But hurry. We must not keep the Son waiting!"

CHAPTER 10

I n the midst of the middle valley that linked the highest heaven with the green land of Gabriel's birth, there was a tree so enormous that it straddled both the river and the highway that ran the length of paradise. All those who traveled up and down the highway, passed between the sturdy roots of that tree, as though they passed through a mammoth tunnel. Gabriel had seen the tree from above, as he, Lucifer and the other archangels had flown across the valley.

From the vantage point of the air above, the tree appeared like an island all its own, so thick was its foliage. Its hundreds of limbs were home to innumerable birds and furry creatures, and twelve different kinds of fruit hung from its branches. Its leaves were every color and shape, velvety, smooth, shiny, iridescent, and flowers of countless descriptions bloomed eternally on its golden twigs.

The river that ran between its sprawling trunks originated from the throne room itself. Likewise, all the pools and ponds of heaven, the myriad streams and fountains, were supplied by this fabulous flood, which was called the River of Life.

The citizens of heaven watered their own gardens and cooked their own household food in that pristine liquid; all food in heaven was life-perpetuating because it had been nurtured by that healthful water.

The tree that straddled the river was, likewise, called the Tree of Life, for it was nourished by the same waters.

It was to this tree that Lucifer and his companions had been summoned.

The conveyance in which they rode was glorious. While it would have been possible for them to fly to their destination with their own wings, or even to wish themselves there with a thought, heaven was the realm of pleasant experiences and, to Gabriel's mind, a ride in this wonderful chariot must surely be one of heaven's finest treats.

The conveyance fairly skimmed over the ground, pulled at a rapid clip by a team of magnificent animals, which Gabriel knew immediately to be horses. He wondered what it would be like to ride on of these creatures, but, for now, the air streaming through his hair and the joy of speed and power were thrilling enough.

As they rolled over hills and dales toward the gigantic tree, Gabriel once again pondered the meaning of the words *the Son*. While it was a beautiful designation, it seemed a bit aloof, and he wondered if he had another, more personal name.

At last, the chariot headed down a slope, the

colossal tree visible in the distance. As they drew closer, the passengers could make out an amazing gathering between the expansive roots on one side. Surrounding a central character, whom Gabriel took to be the Son, was an entourage of attendants, all dressed in gleaming white tunics, some sitting astride more magnificent horses, yet, and others standing guard. The Son, as well, sat upon one of these majestic beasts, which was a good four hands taller than the others, its flowing mane and tail of vivid white and its stamping hooves a gleaming silver.

Almost before they knew it, the conveyance came to a stop on a small rise near the tree. The guardians who had fetched the archangels from Lucifer's mansion climbed out of the vehicle and bade the others do likewise.

Gabriel thought his knees would buckle, throwing him face-first to the ground, as he stepped out. He was about to enter, again, into the presence of divinity, and he was not sure he would be able to stand up. Nor was he certain he *should* stand in the presence of the Son. It would be so natural to fall down, a relief to his awestruck heart.

The guardians, though profoundly reverent in their demeanor, walked with confidence toward their master. Gabriel and the others attempted to do likewise, but when, at last, they were caught by the Son's direct gaze, their strength fled them, and, one by one, they went down, prostrate.

As Gabriel lay before the majesty of the Prince of Heaven, a shudder of great wings was heard overhead. Before he had a chance to identify the source, he was snatched upright, and set firmly on his feet. Each of his companions was treated similarly until the four archangels were clustered together in a wavering huddle, trying to keep their bearings, and Lucifer stood apart, his head bowed.

With a blast of ascent, the same seraph who had greeted them with the tongs and the fiery coal in the throne room, hovered over them. It was he who had stood them upright, and he was ready to right them, should they fall again.

So, here they were, face to face with the Son of God!

When they had first seen him in the throne room, he had been nearly indistinguishable from the Father. In a manner that defied explanation and description, both he and the entity who had leaned upon the back of the Father's throne had been one with God himself.

Now, outside the throne room, the Son was clearly his own person, yet his majesty and the wonder he evoked were not diminished.

He was unsurpassably beautiful. Tall and graceful, he sat upon his fabulous steed with a dignity that emanated pure power. His snow white hair hung to his saddle-back in thick waves, two intricate braids caught back at the temples to form a tiara entwined with gold. Despite his snowy hair, his face, while containing all the eons of heaven, seemed ageless, eternally youthful.

His clothing, while utterly elegant, was simple and straightforward. A gown of blazing white was topped by a sleeveless coat of sky blue, and draping all was a cloak of deep, dark scarlet, its ample hood spread out across his shoulders. Everything was trimmed with gold and silver braid, gleaming gems of many colors peeking here and there from the folds.

His horse's tack was fabulous, all of embossed gold and cushioned wood, carved with dazzling intricacy.

But, they had only a moment to take all of this in, before the prince saluted them with an outstretched arm.

"Good day, friends," he hailed them. "We meet again."

Gabriel's heart lurched. He would have returned the salutation, but his voice failed him. Supporting one another, the four archangels were determined not to fall down. But, it was no use. They simply had no strength to stay upright.

Besides, they were overcome with the desire to worship this mighty prince. Slumping to the ground, even the most self-assured of them, Lucifer, was brought to his knees.

Again, the seraph flew over them, this time raising them to their feet without laying a hand on them. A swift flick of his fingers, and they were upright, once again.

By the time they had regained their composure, the prince had dismounted and was walking toward one root of the mammoth tree. "Follow me," he said, waving them forward. "It is time for us to have a talk."

Michael was the first to comply. Gabriel followed, with Raphael and Uriel close behind, all of them tingling from head to toe. As for Lucifer, he obeyed, independent of the others.

As if he were merely one of them, the prince took a seat upon the ground, leaning against the huge root that rose like a chair-back behind Him. Gesturing toward the grassy space at his feet, he indicated they should join him.

The instant he sat down, his attendants scurried about, preparing a tasty repast for the visitors and for their lord. This would be the second meal Gabriel had ever eaten.

This time, the food was of a more common sort than the cake served in the throne room. Clean white cloths were spread upon the ground, and golden platters, arranged with cheeses and fruits, were set before them. Coarse breads and red wine completed the menu.

The instant the meal was served, the mood

among the guests changed from one of speechless wonder to one of comfort and camaraderie. Their attention swung back and forth between the joys of the taste palate and the joy of the prince's company.

The host put the guests at ease by addressing them each by name. The very way he said Gabriel, Michael, Raphael and Uriel made them feel he knew them better than they knew themselves. And when he referred to Lucifer, his smile was especially broad.

"I have known Son of the Morning for a long while," he said, nodding to the dark- haired angel. "I asked him to be on hand when you took your first breaths. I trust he has been showing you some of the finer points of life in our pleasant land."

Lucifer sat a little straighter at the mention of his duties. It was apparent he took it as a commendation.

Gabriel was the first to endorse his mentor. "I would have been lost without him," he said. "He taught me how to fly!"

Michael and the others could not deny that Lucifer had attended to their first steps admirably.

As the prince had been speaking, several of the little animals who lived in the great tree had crept down the branches. Squirrels with long, fluffy tails hopped toward him, birds flitted from limb to limb, one even daring to light on his shoulder. The prince held up his finger and let the feathered creature step onto it, lifted it to his face and ruffled its downy belly with his nose.

Laughing aloud, he sent it flying with a wave of his hand, and then offered a treat from his plate to one of the squirrels, who gingerly took it in its teeth and stored it in its fat cheeks. Again, he laughed, patting the furry clown on its back and shooing it away.

"Well," the prince said, turning his attention to his guests, "I am sure you understand that you were summoned to the throne room today, not only to be apprised of the Father's creative plans, but so that we might have a look at you...check you over, so to speak."

His eyes twinkled, and the four archangels squirmed.

"Oh, you passed with flying colors," the prince assured them. "We all agreed you are some of our finest handiwork, yet! In fact, I am sure you understand that the Father has chosen you to oversee the administration of his New Creation!"

The four looked sideways at one another. So, Lucifer had said rightly! All of them would be working together, overseeing the most astonishing operation of divine will ever to be enacted!

What a swirl of feelings these words set in motion!

Still, the Son was not finished. Turning to Lucifer, he spoke respectfully. "As for you, Son of the Morning, we shall be putting much responsibility on your shoulders. You, my friend, shall be in charge of all your comrades' activities."

At last, the dreaded possibility was established! Grand as it was to be entrusted with such monumental duties, the idea of being Lucifer's underlings was a grim prospect. Whether or not the Son picked up on their feelings, they could not tell. It seemed he did not, for he went on speaking as though nothing was amiss.

"Did you notice the wonderful carpet that runs through the Father's throne room?" he asked.

Of course they had noticed! The broad, dark blue runner had been the first thing they laid eyes on, as they entered the sacred chamber with bent heads. Woven all through the dense azure material were the likenesses of silvery orbs, golden globes, and a thousand sparkling lights. They had been stunned by its intricate beauty, and they had spoken of it later in wonder, not knowing what it depicted.

"That carpet represents the Father's eternal creativity, the thousand stars, suns and planets he has already made by the power of his thought and the will of his love. I suppose he will go on creating, always. But…this latest plan of his…"

Here the Son broke off, his voice halting

over possibilities they could not have fathomed. "This new plan of his is the most amazing of all," he said with a sigh.

The archangels recalled the near cataclysm which had followed the Father's description of the world he would create, a world populated by beings who could choose to love or not to love him! A world in which darkness could reign as easily as light. A world where he would refuse to impose his will!

Gabriel felt the familiar chill go up his spine at the thought of such a place.

For a long while, not another word was spoken. The attendants stopped their eager serving, the animals were quiet in the tree, the angels were lost in thought. Lucifer's gaze wandered far away in private rumination, and the Son studied them all, one by one, as if reading their souls.

Gabriel became anxious. As had happened too often in his short life, he felt the very substance of this magnificent realm, which he was only beginning to know, was on the verge of some dreadful change.

As much to relieve his tension, as to learn something new, he dared to break the silence with a question.

"Your Majesty," he said, his voice a feather, "we were wondering...well, Sir, all of our names have marvelous meanings, as does every word spoken in heaven. We were wondering if we should call you merely Your Majesty...or..."

The Son accepted Gabriel's floundering inquiry. "You want to know my name, do you?"

Gabriel swallowed hard. Was this wrong?

The prince sat back, his hands on his knees. "I have several names. You may call me *Immanuel, Yeshua, Jesus,* to name a few."

The archangels were astonished, knowing instantly the interpretations. The first, Immanuel, did not come as a surprise, for it meant *God with Us.* But the last, Yeshua or Jesus, now this was a name to give pause.

"*God is Salvation,*" Gabriel gasped.

Michael glanced at him, a cloud passing over his face. He need not have told Gabriel his thoughts. Gabriel knew right well he was wondering how there could be any need of salvation, or rescue, or deliverance in this realm.

But then, how could there be a need for *God's Hero, God's Fire* or *God's Comfort* in a world so perfect as heaven? In truth, what need was there for swords and shields and sentries and guards?

They would have asked these questions, except that the Son was now rising from his place on the ground, going to his horse and swinging himself up into the saddle.

"Until we meet again," he called, nudging his steed toward the highway.

As he rode away, his attendants rushing to keep up with him, Gabriel looked to Lucifer for a measure of solace.

But, Lucifer was also going away, back toward the hills that cradled his headquarters.

What choice did any of them have, but to follow him?

CHAPTER 11

he four archangels entered the lobby of Lucifer's headquarters in eager chatter. Their meeting with the Son had infused them with bubbling energy, so that they had flown all the way home, marveling, laughing and conversing even as they flew, about the grandeur of their host and of his plans for them.

They also spoke of Lucifer, and the amazing way in which the Son had commended him. Perhaps the dark-haired angel was not such a riddle, after all. Perhaps he was just as bright and good as he appeared to be.

As they entered the lobby of the magnificent building, they tempered their chatter to a respectful tone. Where was Son of the Morning, anyway?

Leaving the entryway and the main hall that led to the grand sitting room, they rounded a corner and were delighted to see their shields and swords hanging on the wall. For Gabriel, this was an especially welcome surprise. The last time he had seen his armor had been on the green hill where he was born. When Lucifer had taken him to meet the other three archangels, he had forgotten his weapons and had never had opportunity to return for them.

As for Michael, Raphael and Uriel, they had been obliged to leave their gear in the throne room when they went to meet the Father, and they had not had it in mind when they departed that hallowed place.

Here they were, then, four fabulous shields and four mighty swords. To their amazement, other articles hung with them: four gleaming helmets, leggings and vests of shining bronze, gloves and foot coverings...a wardrobe of war gear, ready for...

For *what* were they ready?

And why had they been placed here, now?

Gabriel stepped up to his armor and stroked it lovingly. "Do you know what the words on the shields mean?" he asked his friends.

Michael gazed on his own outfit, pondering the knotted design that wove its way over the shield's surface. "I have not given it any thought," he said.

Gabriel rocked back on his heels and lifted his chin. "It will come," he said. "Just give it a moment."

"Aha!" Raphael cried. *"Glory to the Lord!"*

"That's right!" Gabriel replied. "Amazing, isn't it, how such knowledge is revealed?"

"Like a blazing fire, it comes into our minds!" Uriel added.

"Just when it is needed," Raphael agreed.

But, Michael, while pleased with the interpretation, seemed preoccupied. A look of deep concern had imprinted his face. "Where is Lucifer?" he said. "Let's go see what he is up to."

The four comrades found the dark angel in the opulent dining room of the headquarters. Spread across the great table in the middle of the room was a huge scroll. Son of the Morning pored over it so intently, he did not even hear his companions enter.

Michael cleared his throat and Lucifer glanced up. "Oh, you are here! Very good!" Lucifer said. "Come, come, look at this, will you?"

He swept his hand above the table, his eyes wide. As the others crowded about, gazing on the long parchment, he exclaimed, "This was here when I arrived. See, it is an expansion on the theme of the carpet that runs through the throne room!"

Gabriel leaned in close and examined what appeared to be a map. Scattered across it were pictures of globes, glistening orbs and lights. The paper, itself, was of the same dark blue color as the runner in the throne room, and everything upon it was gold and silver. These depictions were not merely drawn upon the scroll, but they actually twinkled and throbbed with light, as though alive.

There was no readily apparent order to the figures spread across the scroll. But on closer study, it could be seen that many were grouped in clusters, and that within these clusters were other, smaller arrangements. The smallest groupings were centered about single orbs of glistening gold, which refracted light off the particles that swirled about them.

Yes, there was swirling movement, the figures turning and revolving upon the scroll. As the angels watched, the entire layout took on motion, changing as to some silent rhythm, across the paper.

"What is it?" Gabriel cried. "Is this a life form of some type?"

Lucifer's voice was soft with awe. "I believe this is a depiction of the worlds our God has made, much like the carpet in his inner chamber."

"But..." Raphael gulped, "there was no movement on that carpet! See, this is alive!"

"So it is," Lucifer agreed. "Alive, or representative of life. What we are seeing here, my friends, is a record of the courses of stars, suns, moons, galaxies..."

The words tumbled out like notations from a celestial dictionary, words which they could only imagine the meanings of.

"Why," Uriel gasped, "there are thousands upon thousands of lights! What is their purpose? Why does the Father keep creating them, again and again?"

Indeed, as they watched, the scroll seemed to be growing. Ever so slightly did it lengthen, until it began to curl over the table edge, light after light developing along its extremities.

Lucifer stepped to the head of the table and pushed a chair underneath, to catch the growing paper. Reaching the chair seat, one end began to roll over in a coil, which grew fatter by the moment.

"If it does not stop, the entire room will be full of it!" Gabriel cried. "What are we to do?"

As Lucifer rushed to the opposite end of the table, pushing another chair under that end, the same thing happened, until each roll was fat as a hand width.

Michael's face split in a smile. "I think our Father is playing a joke on us!" he laughed.

By now the top and bottom margins of the scroll were beginning to expand, draping over the table sides. Uriel and Raphael rushed to place chairs along the length of the table. "You will not think this so funny when the entire house is taken up!" Uriel cried.

Michael was nearly doubled over with laughter, and Gabriel was so astonished, he was frozen in place.

Then, as quickly as it had begun, the growing stopped. The paper seemed to hum along its edges, the rolls upon the seats quivering for a moment. In a flash, the scroll retracted, its edges shrinking back to their original size, and its ends snapping back to form a double tube, small and tight.

Lucifer was dumbfounded. He stood back gawking at the scroll, until he retrieved his voice.

"This is how I found it," he said. "It was like this, upon the table, when I entered."

Gabriel managed to move, daring to step a little closer to the scroll. "Did you open it, yourself, or did it open of its own accord?" he asked.

"It was tied with a silver cord," Lucifer said. "See?" He reached into his robe and pulled out a thin silver rope. "I removed this and unrolled the scroll."

The angels were very quiet, fearing to breathe. They each knew what the others were thinking. Should they dare to open the scroll, again?

"Go ahead, Lucifer," Michael said. "Open it."

"I think not," Lucifer replied. "I think it best to leave it alone."

Again, they stood by silently, wondering what to do.

"Do you really think it's dangerous?" Gabriel asked. "Go ahead, Michael, open it."

"Me?" Michael wheezed, pointing to his

chest. "Why me? You are *God's Hero*, Gabriel. You open it!"

This was a taunt, as much as a command. But, Gabriel took no offense. It seemed none of his friends was going to do anything. So, he took courage.

Stepping to the table, he reached forth a quivering hand, once, twice, fearful of touching the living thing. He could feel his comrades' eyes upon him.

Taking a quick breath, he closed his own eyes and stretched out one hand, then the other. Grasping the two coils, he parted them, and, instantly, the whole thing unraveled.

Gabriel jumped back, wishing his armor was with him and not hanging on a peg in the hall.

As the scroll spread, again, across the table, they found that the scene upon it had changed. Now there were only a few stars upon the cobalt surface, much larger and more distinct than those depicted before. As the angels peered down upon it, Raphael noted, "This appears to be a small corner of the previous design. I think something is about to happen here."

As they watched, a tiny quadrant of blue space seemed to darken, a hazy mass undulating upon it and growing in size until it pushed at the edges of adjacent stars.

There it sat, just like that, unchanging,

except for the surging and heaving, the ebbing and swelling of the dark mass.

"What can it mean?" Uriel marveled. "What does this strange void represent?"

Gabriel thought back to the lesson staged in the throne room, the moment when all went dark, overwashed with pure blackness, a swimming cauldron of inky emptiness. And he remembered the question which the Father had put to them.

"What if somewhere, in some way, the light ceased to shine, or never shone in the first place? What if light were to come upon a place as though never before existing, and what if the darkness fought to overcome it?"

"I think...I think..." Gabriel struggled for the right words. "Perhaps we are being given a glimpse of our Father's new project. At least, its crudest beginnings."

The others agreed, but, were still bewildered.

"Why?" Uriel asked. "Why are we so privileged?"

Michael looked at Lucifer, who was already caught away in furtive imaginings. "According to the Son, this is *our* project, as well the Father's," Michael said. "I think we will be called into action, very soon."

CHAPTER 12

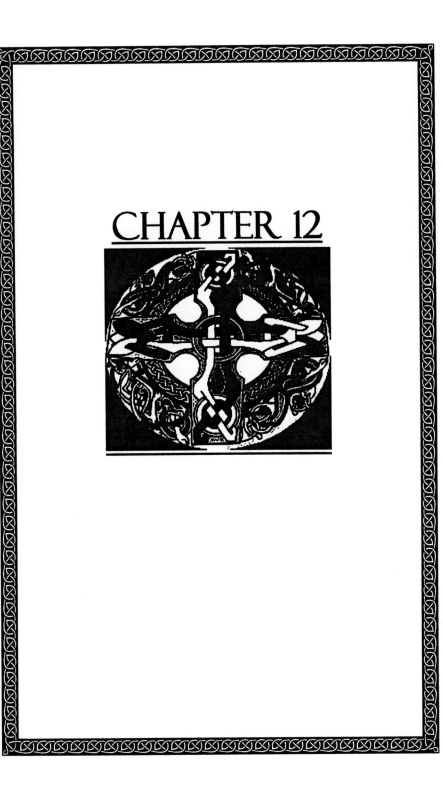

I t seemed an awfully long time intervened before Michael's prediction came true. The four archangels grew bored with arranging and rearranging the furnishings in the headquarters, tending the gardens outside and waiting.

Lucifer spent most of his time hunched over the map, watching the seething mass that was growing in one corner. Gabriel often walked by him, as he ran some errand, and longed to ask him what he was thinking, what it was about the strange, pulsing void that so mesmerized him.

Once, when he dared to pause and look over Lucifer's shoulder, he saw that the dark angel held his hand just inches above the hazy mass, as though attempting to communicate with it. To Gabriel's amazement, streaks of fiery light shot through the mass as Lucifer did this, small, jagged bolts of pure energy.

What phenomenon was this? It seemed Lucifer had a special connection to the enigma, a personal bond. When Gabriel witnessed this, he backed away, tiptoeing out of the room without Lucifer so much as looking up.

Often, after that, Gabriel and his three closer friends had discussed this mystery. Uriel seemed to have the best explanation. "The Son said that

Lucifer would be overseeing all our work on this project. Perhaps the Father has gifted him with a unique cognitive link to the place."

They had left it at that, though they pondered the implications many times between themselves.

There was another troubling change following the advent of the scroll. The entire valley and all the heavenlies seemed to have focused interest on their headquarters. Daily, as they worked about the grounds, or glanced out the windows and arches of the place, they saw passersby on the highway below stop to gaze up at their palace. Sometimes whole groups of them came out from the cities and villages, hoping to witness activity up their way.

It was clear that news of the Son's visit and his words to them had been spread far and wide throughout the realm. The citizens of the kingdom were not an ignorant lot. They had put two and two together: the pronouncement made by the Father, which shook the foundations of heaven, and the instructions the Son had given Lucifer, were intertwined. Whatever the nature of the project which the Father was about to undertake, the four archangels, with Lucifer at the head, were central to it.

The Great Experiment was the most profound of mysteries, and one which all the angels of heaven desired to look into.

At last, there was a break in the tedium.

Gabriel was pruning a pear tree in Lucifer's garden, one of a dozen varieties of fruit trees that were scattered about the grounds. For a little while, as he enjoyed this work, his heart had been less heavy, his thoughts free of concern for what the future held and what his mentor might be up to. Suddenly, however, he was jolted by the sound of horses' hooves on the cobblestone path leading to the palace.

Laying down his pruning shears, he rounded the front of the house and saw a lesser angel approaching, leading four wonderful creatures by their reins. One sorrel horse, one palomino, one bay and one silver-gray pranced behind him. "Greetings, Master Gabriel," the visitor said. "Are your brothers about?"

"Michael, Raphael and Uriel are in the back garden," he replied. "Lucifer is inside."

Gabriel's eyes were glued to the horses. "What wonderful animals!" he exclaimed. "May I?" He held out his hand, offering the palomino horse a sprig of grass.

"You have every right, sir," the angel answered. "These horses are for you and the other archangels."

Gabriel was amazed. "Wonderful!" he cried. "But, what need do we have of horses? And, what of Lucifer? Will he have one?"

The angel tied the horses' reins to a nearby bush, reached into his cloak and drew out a small scroll. Bowing, he handed it to Gabriel, then said, "This should answer your questions, Master. I shall now be going."

At this, the visitor turned away and hastened down the cobblestone path, leaving Gabriel in silent wonder.

Just as he was opening the scroll, his three friends approached, having come in search of him. "What's happening?" Michael asked, amazed to see the glorious creatures on the path.

"A courier from the throne room was just here," he replied, noting the address on the scroll. *From the Inner Sanctum*, said the inscription. "He brought these horses and this message," he explained, showing them the scroll.

Raphael stepped up to the bay horse and stroked his velvety nose. Uriel patted the gray horse on his dappled neck, and Michael stood in awe before the sorrel, whose coloring was much like his own. In fact, it did not escape them that each horse was color coordinated with a specific owner.

"Read it," Michael implored. "Tell us what it says!"

Gabriel tingled as he unrolled the little paper. Emblazoned across the top was the likeness of the Lord's carpet, a streak of cobalt blue ink upon the parchment, with stars sprinkled across it. Beneath were the words: *"To the Four Archangels: Michael, Gabriel, Uriel and Raphael."*

Gabriel swallowed hard and looked at his comrades. "It…it leaves out Lucifer," he stammered.

They had not missed this fact, as they leaned in close, their wide eyes scanning the greeting. "Go on," Michael spurred him.

Gabriel unrolled the scroll yet further, and read aloud:

"The presentation of these wonderful steeds denotes the beginning of your mission. As Master Lucifer stays behind to aid in the management of my New Creation, your first duty shall be to enlist other governors in a great celebration. To the far corners of the heavens, from planet to planet, star to star, proclaim that the Lord is about to do a new thing, a thing such as has never been done in all of eternity past. Call forth praise from the realms of light, command the stars to welcome the dawning of the New Creation. For as they rejoice, the sound of their symphony shall echo the works of my hands and bless the advent of this New Day. Go forth then, each on a different path, and be my holy heralds. Your Father."

Hands shaking, Gabriel rolled up the scroll

again, his eyes closed. For a long while, the four archangels were silent. At last, Raphael voiced the question that filled their hearts:

"How are we to do this? Where do we start? Where do we go?"

Michael stroked the muscular neck of his scarlet horse. "Maybe it will come to us, just as other things have. Like the meaning of the words on our shields. Maybe, once we mount these beasts, we will simply know. We will turn their heads in the right directions, and we will just go."

Uriel quivered. "And what will we say when we get where we are going?"

Before anyone else answered, he laughed. "Very well…we will *just know*!"

The others nodded.

Gabriel glanced furtively toward the house. "So, do we say good-bye to Lucifer? Do we just ride away, without a word?"

Michael shrugged. "If Lucifer cares what becomes of us, he will leave his precious map and see us off."

Raphael had a more pressing question. "But, what of our armor? Should we go inside and get it?"

To their amazement, Lucifer appeared on the porch right then. "What need have you of armor, on such a journey?" he called.

They did not know how to answer. They had

never understood the need of armor at any time.

"What you need is speed!" Lucifer cried. "Away, now, fellows! The void on the map is full of chaos. I think the New Creation is about to begin!"

CHAPTER 13

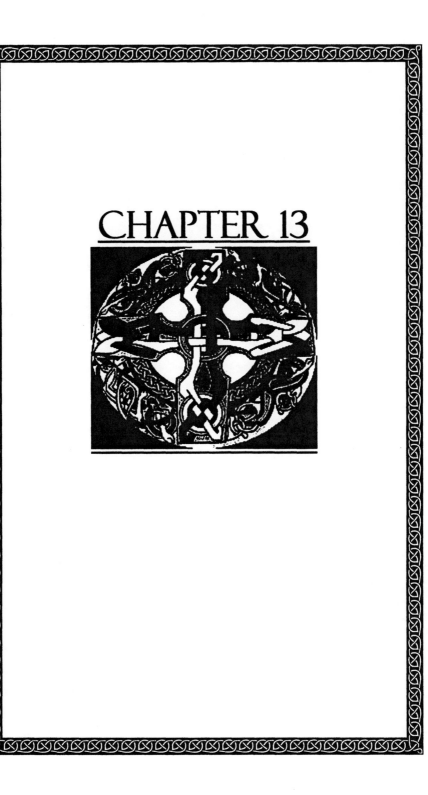

he fingers of Gabriel's right hand intertwined with his horse's flaxen mane in a knotty braid. His palms sweated, and he wished he had not left his sword behind. Bent tight against the creature's back, he wrapped his left arm under its powerful neck and held on tight.

The instant he had climbed into the saddle, the horse had bolted skyward, and it had not slowed down, though he commanded it to do so over and over. The animal definitely had a mind of its own. Bent on some destination unknown to the rider, it shot through the heavens like a golden dart.

For a long while, Gabriel feared to look about him as he hurtled through space. When he did open his eyes, he saw countless fiery suns and marbled planets speeding past, stars and moons of a hundred descriptions. It occurred to him that he journeyed within the reality which the Lord's carpet and Lucifer's map only symbolized. When his horse would stop and where, he had no idea.

The last time he had seen his three companions, they, too, had just mounted their steeds. Like his, the other horses had shot skyward, each taking off for a different corner of the universe. Like lightning, the glistening heralds had lit out for unknown parts, to give a message unrehearsed.

"Whoa, you crazy animal! Whoa, Baraq!" The name he had given his horse had leapt to mind just as so many words had done. The meaning, *flashing arrow*, suited the creature's headstrong disregard for its master's wishes.

This time, however, the horse seemed to hear him. Either that, or it had just reached its destination, and would have slowed down, anyway.

As Gabriel pulled back on the reins, the creature glided to the surface of a misty world.

"Very good!" the rider cried.

The horse turned his head and stared at him, as if to ask why he had been shouting. The rider swung himself out of the saddle and stroked the horse's soft nose. "I apologize," he said. "It just seemed you had lost your head, as though you would go on forever."

The horse snorted and stamped the ground softly, indicating that he had known where he was going. The angel of the throne room, the one with the fiery tongs, had told him precisely where to go.

Gabriel turned about, surveying the place on which they had landed. "So, where exactly are we?" he asked. "And where do we go from here?"

As Baraq shook his mane free of the knot his master had put in it, the corner of a parchment worked up from one saddlebag. The archangel, wondering what this could be, drew it out, and was surprised to find it a smaller version of the map that filled Lucifer's dining room table.

As if in answer to his first question, one of the smaller planets on the surface began to give off a throbbing glow. Gabriel drew the paper close and squinted at the light. Beneath it, in cryptic letters, was the word *Kinnowr*.

Gabriel scratched his head. *Kinnowr,* he thought. *Home of the harp and lyre.*

Baraq snorted again, and began to walk into the depths of a dark wood. It seemed he was replying to his master's second question, but Gabriel thought he read impatience in the horse's gait. *You are the master. I got you here, but I cannot fulfill your mission,* he seemed to be saying.

Gabriel was astonished at his animal's independence. "Very well," he said. "Wait for me, won't you?"

As he ran to catch up with Baraq, his ears were pricked by the sound of sweet music coming from within or beyond the mist that rose from the dewy ground. Grasping his horse's reins, he followed a path of glistening pebbles that led down a fern-bordered lane.

At last, he emerged into an open meadow, all dappled with tree-shadows and mellow light.

Across the meadow and all along the rolling hills that framed it were small houses, with irregular, straw-thatched roofs and windows lit with the glow of hearth fires. Before each door, within each flower garden, and in patchy groves of evergreens sat young musicians, playing upon harps and lyres of the finest craftsmanship.

"So," he marveled, "this is where the harpists and the lyrists take their training."

As he led Baraq into the clearing, he was not far from one especially accomplished gathering.

"Very well, youngsters," their director addressed them. "Soon you will be ready to join the singers of Shiyr and..."

Here his students chimed in, reciting the familiar refrain: *And from there to work with the psalmists of Zamiyr...and from there..."*

Suddenly they stopped, following their director's wide-eyed gaze. He had caught sight of Gabriel and Baraq where they stood at the edge of the misty forest.

Such a picture the visitor made in this quaint place, emerging like a vision from the woodland depths. Gabriel, with his golden hair and shining robe, his powerful wings, and imposing stature: they knew immediately that he was a superior angel!

The music teacher bowed. "Good day, sir,"

he said with a stammer, his long, thin fingers tugging at his wispy goatee. "To what do we owe the honor of your presence?"

Though all the music of the hamlet had ceased and all eyes were on him, Gabriel was suddenly at ease.

"Good day," he replied. "But, please, do not stop. I was enjoying your work."

Here and there, other teachers raised their batons, but the resultant clamor was discordant.

The director shifted his diminutive body tensely, and rolled his eyes in the direction of the other groups. "Uh, they are a bit nervous, my lord. Is there something we may do for you?"

Gabriel draped his horse's reins over a tree branch and sat down upon a rock. "Go on about the singers and the psalmists," he said. "I did not mean to interrupt."

The director fidgeted with his baton. "We…we were just reminding ourselves of our goals."

"I see," Gabriel said. "Your students advance from here to other schools?"

"Yes," the director replied. "On Shiyr…"

"*Home of the singers,*" Gabriel interpreted.

"Yes, yes," the director answered. "You understand. Then, on to Zamiyr…"

"*Home of the psalmists.*"

"Why, yes, sir!" the director enthused,

155

flashing a big smile.

Gabriel was beginning to understand the process. "These places are more than hamlets," he guessed.

The director was bemused. "Why yes, of course, sir. They are realms of their own…planets, in fact. Just like…"

"Just like Kinnowr."

"Exactly," the director said. "But, then, you surely knew all of this." His brow knit as though the archangel toyed with him.

Gabriel had *not* known, but he was not about to admit that to this underling. He imagined that his fellow archangels must be paying calls on other sorts of worlds, and he smiled as he envisioned them being thrust into strange and distant places, with no preparation.

"So," he went on, quizzing the director, "when the harpists, the singers and the psalmists complete their training, do they go straight to join the seraphim?"

The students looked as though a joke were being played on them. One of them shot a hand into the air. "Of course not, sir!" he answered. "Not until we are selected for a choir on *Towdah*."

One of the more feminine musicians joined in, "And if we are not selected, we return for more training."

Towdah, Gabriel thought. *Home of the*

choirs.

Now he understood why his horse had been groomed to carry him here, and why, undoubtedly, Michael, Uriel and Raphael had been sent to sister planets where music was the main occupation.

The director stood silent for a moment, wondering what Gabriel was thinking. He did not know whether he should speak again, but he knew his students must be getting hungry after hours of practice.

He cleared his throat once more. "Master, it is time for the session to end. The students should be going home."

Gabriel must fulfill his purpose, but it was not going quite as he had imagined. He had foreseen himself hovering over mighty realms, shouting in a voice that filled the heavens, "Prepare ye! Prepare ye! The Father requires your service!"

Or some such thing.

Instead, he was speaking one on one with a rather insignificant looking fellow, a music teacher who was anxious to release a bunch of students for the afternoon.

Gabriel stepped up to the smaller angel and, feeling a bit awkward, called him aside for a private word. "I have been sent to tell you that the Father is about to do a new thing."

Suddenly, the teacher brightened. "Oh, yes,

we have heard of that!" he exclaimed. "The New Creation…it is all the buzz out here."

Gabriel was chagrined. Any glory he thought to take in this mission was being steadily stripped from him. But, as he considered this, it occurred to him just how silly such pride would be. Everything he was and everything he possessed had been given by the Father's hand. What had he to glory in?

Strangely, the revelation came as a relief. His face broke into another smile.

"Well, sir, you will be glad to know that our God requires your service. At the dawning of this New Creation, he wishes for all the musicians, psalmists and choirs of the universe to participate."

The teacher was astonished. "Truly?" he marveled. "What an honor! We will be delighted to help where we can."

Gabriel nodded. "When the time is right, you will know. Have your students prepare the grandest arrangement they know. And, oh yes, pass the word, won't you?"

The teacher was thrilled. "Indeed, indeed, I shall!"

As Gabriel turned to leave, the smaller fellow hastened to share the news with his students. But Gabriel thought again.

"Uh, sir," he called after him, "are there

many planets of music, other than the ones you have already named?"

The teacher was incredulous. Was it possible this archangel really did not know these things?

"Oh, hundreds, sir! Thousands, surely!" he replied. "Do you intend to visit them all?"

CHAPTER 14

he Father certainly had a way of putting things in perspective, Gabriel thought, as he guided his horse back through the woods to the place where they had touched down. Never again would he presume to know how things should go, how God would use him or what lessons could come from the simplest of encounters.

He had learned, from his visit to the hamlet, that the Father did not always act in mighty flourishes, with thunder and lightning. He had learned that to be a herald was not to attract glory to oneself, but to be an obedient messenger, in sometimes humble places.

He hoped to store such lessons in his heart, so that he would remember them always.

Accepting the idea that being an archangel was not always glamorous, he was surprised to find, when he went to mount his horse, that something prestigious had been added to his equipment. A stunning silver trumpet hung from his saddle horn by a scarlet cord.

Blinking his eyes, he marveled at the instrument, wondering if it meant what he thought it might. Fearful of touching it, he managed to lift one finger and quickly trace the letters engraved upon its side. *Glory to the Lord*, it said.

"Just like my shield!" he exclaimed. "Baraq, do you know what this is for?"

Baraq was intent on nibbling sweet grass at his hooves.

Gabriel lifted the trumpet from the saddle and ran his hand along its slick stem. "Perhaps there is a place for grand entrances in this line of work," he said. "How could anyone blow upon such a trumpet humbly?"

Baraq glanced up at him, looking quite content to be in his presence. It seemed Gabriel had passed more than one test, today.

Joy sprang up in the archangel's heart. Swinging himself into the saddle, he patted his horse on the withers. "Very well, then!" he cried. "Let's be off!"

What must have been a very long time passed quickly as Gabriel and Baraq journeyed from planet to planet in the Father's universe, stopping at those which the map indicated were the homes of music and musicians.

Often, when the archangel gave his message, it was with trumpet blasts that rocked the foundations of worlds. "Prepare! Prepare! The Father is about to do a new thing! Singers, musicians, arise! Hone your skills and make ready to celebrate the dawn of a New Day!"

Just as many times, he was impressed to

touch down on unknown soil, to go seeking just the right contact, and to give his message in private encounters. Always, however, he told those he met to help spread the word, and always they were eager to comply.

He had no idea how long he had been away, when Baraq turned, at last, for home.

The realm of heaven glowed with the light that had no equal, the light that shown forth from the City Celeste, whose source was the Son of God. Such a welcome sight his own valley was; even the headquarters where Lucifer resided was inviting!

The palatial residence was still tiny in the distance and the homecomers were still aloft, when Gabriel dismounted, unfurled his wings and flew beside his horse until they were ready to touch down. This maneuver he had perfected along his journey, sometimes leaving Baraq far behind and proclaiming his message to worlds below as though he were a solitary star.

The air of heaven was sweet against his face, somehow far sweeter than even the purest air of the many planets he had visited. How good to be home!

He wondered if the other archangels had yet returned, and if it would be inappropriate to announce his own arrival with a blast on his silver trumpet.

He had become quite accomplished with this instrument. The first time he had lifted it to his lips, and had blown into it, Baraq and he had been in a wide open stretch of space, well away from Kinnowr. The squawking sound had made his horse bolt and had caused Gabriel to cringe with embarrassment.

But, with a little practice, he had gotten the hang of it, and now could not imagine being without his trumpet.

Why not surprise his friends with a few notes of greeting? He unwound the scarlet cord from his saddle horn and was just about to announce his arrival, when he noticed a crowd gathered on the road and hillside outside the headquarters. It seemed some auspicious event was about to take place, as the citizens of the valley milled about and eagerly spoke in animated conversation, glancing repeatedly toward the house.

Gabriel returned his trumpet to its place and clucked his tongue, causing Baraq to slow down. "Let's land here," he said, pointing to a grove a short distance from the headquarters. "We can walk the rest of the way."

The horse and master avoided the throng, keeping within the shadows of the grove. When they had come within a few feet of the veranda that encircled the house, a voice called softly but urgently through the trees. "Gabriel! We are here! Come join us!"

It was Michael, who stood hidden with Raphael and Uriel in the thick bowers nearest the building. "What took you so long?" Michael muttered. "We were beginning to think you would never come!"

Gabriel shrugged. "Have I missed anything?" he asked.

Raphael sighed impatiently. "For days now, Lucifer has been drawing unseemly attention to himself."

"Days?" Gabriel gasped. "When did you return."

Michael shook his head. "Never mind. It appears you must have had more places to visit than we did. We have all been home quite a while."

"Yes," Uriel agreed. "And we could have used your assistance. Lucifer's attitude is getting out of hand!"

Raphael leaned close to Gabriel and spoke in urgent tones. "Every evening, just as citizens are returning home along the highway, Lucifer has been appearing on the veranda. He says little…just stands there, soaking up the admiration of the crowds."

"But, why? What do they see in him that they have not seen before?" Gabriel asked.

Uriel blew through clenched teeth. "It all started with that cloak of his!" Then, remembering that Gabriel had been away, "Oh, but, you have not seen it, have you?"

Raphael rolled his eyes. "As if Lucifer did not have enough to build himself up! First he is given command of this New Project, and then he is given the map..."

"Over which he gloats day in and out," Michael interjected.

"And now," Uriel finished, "he finds this confounded cloak in his closet! What can the Father be thinking?"

"The Father?" Gabriel said. "The Father gave him a cloak?"

"Apparently!" Michael exclaimed. "It seems we have all been graced with some special gift. Mine was a breastplate of iron. See?" Michael pulled his robe aside, revealing an impenetrable coat of mail.

"And mine a goblet, filled with healing herbs," Raphael said. At this, he drew the golden cup from a his long sleeve, capped with a silver lid.

"As for me, I have been given the gift of fire, so that when I touch my sword it blazes with flaming light," Uriel said.

Gabriel turned to Baraq, and pointed out the shining trumpet hanging on the saddle. "This is why I was so long coming," he said. "I must have traveled to more planets than any of you, for I have been given the gift of proclamation."

Michael smiled. "So, *God's Hero* is now also *God's Messenger*," he said. "You are a fellow of many talents!"

The four laughed together, but then Gabriel grew somber. "So, what of Lucifer? Tell me about this cloak of his."

Just as Gabriel said this, the crowd in front of the house grew noisier.

"Watch!" Michael said. "You will see for yourself, soon enough."

Within moments, Son of the Morning appeared, and stood dramatically on the porch, soaking in the praise of the onlookers. Draped over his shoulders and spread in dazzling folds to the floor, was the most magnificent robe any of them had ever seen.

Gabriel blinked his eyes as Lucifer turned this way and that in the light of Heaven, the jewels of his robe throwing off a kaleidoscope of colors.

"It must have every precious stone ever created!" Michael marveled. "Rubies, sapphires, diamonds..."

"Emeralds, jasper, onyx..." Raphael added.

"And it is all laced with silver and gold!" Uriel said.

"But, why?" Gabriel groaned. "Why does he

deserve this?"

No one answered, before the crowd grew quiet. It appeared Lucifer was about to speak, taking a step toward the railing and stretching his arms wide.

"Children of God!" he cried, his deep voice resonating through the hills. "All things are ready! Yesterday we were still waiting to hear that all the worlds our Father has created have been put on notice of his Grand Plan. Today, our emissary Gabriel, has at last returned. We are ready to commence!"

A mighty shout and applause rang up the hillside. Gabriel felt the eyes of Lucifer upon him, as he had spotted him in the trees. His throat went dry when Son of the Morning hailed him forth.

"Come, come, God's Hero! Let us all hear about your adventures!"

Michael and the others avoided Gabriel's hot gaze. "You did not tell me I would have to do this!" he said. "Come with me!"

Michael gave a hollow laugh. "No, friend," he said. "We have had our moment in the arena. It's your turn."

His friends pushed him forward, into plain view, and Gabriel stumbled up the steps.

Lucifer greeted him warmly, as the crowd shouted his name over and over. "Gabriel, Gabriel, God's Hero!"

Gabriel leaned close to Lucifer and whispered, "I really have nothing to say. Just get on with it!"

He stepped away, ready to leave the stage, but Lucifer grabbed his sleeve and drew him back.

"So, Gabriel," he announced, "word has it that you and your fellow emissaries have succeeded in spreading the word. Tell us, what sorts of places did you visit?"

Gabriel turned awkwardly to the eager crowd, and cleared his throat. "I, uh…my duty was to enlist the help of the celestial choirs in ushering in the New Creation."

His tension was somewhat alleviated when the crowd broke into spontaneous applause. Still, he felt uneasy with it. Lucifer, on the other hand, seemed to revel in it, as though he, and not Gabriel, had fulfilled the mission.

Lowering his head, Gabriel felt a pang of shame. He had done nothing wrong, but it grieved him to be absorbed by Lucifer's glory.

As Lucifer bowed to the crowd, Gabriel stealthily slipped away, creeping into the entryway of the headquarters. No one seemed to notice, so taken were they with the wonder of the Morning Son. Gabriel had never wept before, had never seen tears upon anyone's face. But his heart was pounding and his throat tightened with the beginning of sorrow.

He did not understand this new emotion, could not analyze it. He only knew that, as he heard the rising chant of the crowd outside, the feeling intensified.

"Lucifer, Son of the Morning! Full of wisdom! Perfect in beauty! Lucifer, Son of the Morning, Prince of the New Creation!"

Suddenly, another, even more powerful emotion welled up in him. Sorrow was replaced by the yearning to feel his sword in his hand. This inscrutable feeling frightened him, yet he found himself drawn toward the rack where he had seen his armor hanging.

As he made his way down the eerie corridor, he was aware that the entire house had a different feeling than he remembered. It had always been a cold, intimidating place. But, now it was imbued throughout with a sense of gloom.

He remembered feeling this way when entering Lucifer's map room. Now, it seemed, that ominous mood dwelled in every wall and piece of furniture.

Then he heard unfamiliar voices echoing through the hall.

He rounded the last corner leading to the armor rack and was taken aback to find a huddle of brawny angels gathered there. They did not notice him, as he came toward them, so engrossed were they in admiring the shields and weaponry on the wall.

"What are the words engraved here?" he heard one say. "What do they mean?"

"They mean *Glory to The Lord*," Gabriel announced, as he wedged his way between the burly strangers, to stand protectively between them and the armor.

He had seen these fellows before. They were of the warrior contingent he had observed when he was first aware of the world about him. They had been created on the same day as he and his fellow archangels, and he had been impressed by them that morning on the green hill, just as he was now.

"Captain Gabriel!" one of them cried. Suddenly they all straightened, saluting him as though he were their commander.

He smiled nervously. "At ease, fellows," he said. "I am not your captain."

They looked askance at one another. "Oh, but, sir...yes, you are! Master Lucifer has told us so! You, and Michael and the others...you are all our captains. We stand ready to obey you, in Lucifer's service."

Gabriel had no time to question what they meant, before the sound of other voices, dozens and dozens of them, issued through the rooms and hallways of the house.

Soon, the tramping of feet brought a horde of warrior angels into the corridor, their hands at the ready on the hilts of their sheathed swords.

"It is all right!" the first warrior cried. "It is Captain Gabriel."

The oncomers skidded to a halt in front of the weapon rack. Gabriel thought he read disappointment in their faces, that he was not some intruder.

"Who are all of you?" Gabriel cried. "What service does Lucifer require, that demands swords and warriors?"

But, before they could reply, Michael appeared behind them, head and shoulders taller than them all.

His red face glowering, he sent them scurrying off in all directions. "Away!" he ordered, leaving Gabriel shaking against the wall.

By now, Raphael and Uriel had also arrived, making for the most welcome sight Gabriel had ever seen.

"What is going on?" he cried. "What are these warriors doing here?"

Michael looked knowingly at the other two and then, placing a hand on Gabriel's shoulder, he led him down the hall. "Let's find a quiet place to talk," he said. "We have much to tell you."

CHAPTER 15

t was not easy to find a quiet place to talk, as Michael had suggested. Every nook had been taken over by Lucifer's new residents. Not only did warriors come and go, but masons and carpenters worked hours each day expanding and embellishing the headquarters.

"What about our own rooms?" Gabriel asked. "Surely our private quarters have not been invaded."

"Good idea," Michael said. "Let's go into my suite."

They were about to comply, when Gabriel stopped still. "I don't know if it *is* such a good idea," he said. "There are too many ears in this place. Besides, I left my horse in the bower. I had better look after him."

"We have been spending a lot of time outside," Uriel said, as they made their way back to the grove. "Things have not been so comfortable in the house."

Gabriel was relieved to find Baraq still standing quietly in the trees, waiting for him. He did not know why he should be concerned for his welfare. He had never had cause to be concerned for anyone's welfare in this realm of peace.

But, things had changed. As Uriel said,

things were not so "comfortable" anymore.

Untying Baraq's rein from the bush where he was tethered, he slapped him gently on the rump. "Go down into the pasture," he commanded. "There is good eating there."

At this, Baraq snorted and galloped happily away.

"Marvelous creatures, aren't they?" Gabriel said. "He was a good companion on my journey."

"Mine, too," Raphael agreed. And the others acknowledged the bravery and speed of their own mounts.

"Even the Son rides a horse!" Uriel recalled. "They must be the noblest of beasts!"

Gabriel's brow knit. "What of Lucifer? Why doesn't he have a horse?"

The archangels shook their heads. "I am sure he could have one, if he wanted," Michael said.

This was spoken with a bite, and Uriel quipped, "It seems Lucifer can have anything he wants."

Gabriel rubbed his chin anxiously. "So, let's get to the point, comrades. Just what is Lucifer up to?"

The three looked at one another, and at last Michael approached the conclusion they had all come to, in Gabriel's long absence. "Son of the Morning claims that all these warriors who are hanging about are here in service to the project. He claims he has given them strict orders to obey all our commands and to get ready for any work the Father's New Creation requires."

Gabriel studied Michael's doubtful expression. "You are not convinced that is all there is to it."

"Are you?" Michael laughed.

Gabriel's silence spoke for him.

Uriel nudged Raphael, who tensed beside him. "Go ahead!" he said, seeing Raphael's clenched fists. "Tell him."

"What?" Gabriel muttered through his teeth. "Tell me what?"

Raphael swallowed. "A few days ago, I found Lucifer hunched over his map..."

"As he most always is!" Uriel interjected.

"He did not see me enter..."

"You are not so interesting as the map!" Uriel threw in.

Raphael shot his friend a look of aggravation. "Do *you* want to tell this, Uriel?"

Uriel turned his eyes to the ground.

"Anyway," Raphael went on, "he neither saw me nor knew that I was close at hand, when he began to talk to himself...to the map, actually."

Gabriel leaned forward.

"I heard him say something most peculiar...most unsettling..."

"Yes, yes, go on!" Gabriel groaned.

"He was chanting, actually. Over and over, these strange words:

"*We are the Father's dearest love,*

"*O World to Come!*

"*We are as dear to him*

"*As his dearest Son.*"

Gabriel was aghast. Sitting back, he stared at Raphael. "You don't say!" he cried. "Lucifer thinks he is one with the New Creation?"

Raphael nodded. "Apparently so. He equates his sovereignty over this project with the project itself! And not only that…"

Michael could stay still no longer. "He equates himself with the Son!"

Gabriel's face went white. He could barely find his voice, as he put two and two together. "So, Raphael, it is just as you predicted, that day when we sat beside the stream and Lucifer went off to find his headquarters. I shall never forget how you said that Lucifer would not stand still to see the leadership of the New World go to the Son."

He lowered his head, fighting that strange sensation called *sorrow*, which was so new to him. "Oh, how I denied that notion that day! I could not believe anything evil of my dear mentor!"

Michael placed a brotherly hand on Gabriel's knee. "None of us wanted to believe it," he said. "He was our mentor, too."

Gabriel let go a heavy sigh, his shoulders slumped. "Then, we all know why these warriors are lurking about. We know, even if they do not know, themselves. Poor fellows! Lucifer means to use them for no good, just as he would use us!"

Uriel pounded his thigh. "For insurrection!" he cried.

Insurrection! Rebellion! Revolution!

Where did such words come from? How could such possibilities even be conceived, in this perfect world?

Yet, it was happening. There was no doubt.

If the archangels knew what was Good, they could not fail to know what was Evil.

For a long while they sat in morbid silence, each pondering the future's ugliest potentials.

At last, Raphael tried to shake the dread that had settled over them all. Mustering a bit of optimism, he declared, "But, it is not too late! At least we know what is going on. We can surely take a stand, can we not?"

Uriel brightened. "Why, of course! We must take a stand!"

Gabriel watched their enthusiastic gestures, their eager faces, and he recoiled.

"Listen to yourselves!" he interrupted. "See what you are becoming! You speak of *war*, my friends! Can you be any better than Lucifer, in that case?"

Michael studied Gabriel's resistance, and did not approve. "Here you go, again! After all that has happened! You defend your precious Lucifer, even yet!"

Gabriel was appalled. "No, no! You don't understand," he objected. "I do not defend him, or his evil plotting! I only…Oh, I don't know! I just think we should not overreact."

The others were shocked. "*Overreact? Overreact?*" they cried. "You would have us not act at all!"

Michael was the most insistent. Looking straight into his hesitant comrade's eyes, he demanded, "Why do you think we were given swords and shields, if we are never to use them?"

Gabriel felt the first tears of his young life well in his eyes. These tears would become as familiar to him as his own heartbeat, in days to come. He raised a finger to touch them as they spilled over his pallid cheeks.

"Very well," he conceded. "But, before we behave rashly, shouldn't we at least consult with the throne room. The Father and the Son may not have any idea what is going on here."

CHAPTER 16

he archangels' determination to take word of Lucifer's aberrant behavior to the throne room came none too soon. Rest time of the next day had come and gone, the first meal of the day had been completed, and citizens were out on the roads again, going about their business, when Lucifer made his most overt move yet.

Gabriel, Michael, Raphael and Uriel were in the pasture, whistling for their horses, when Lucifer appeared, once again, upon his veranda. He was done up, as usual, in his fabulous garb, his robe casting a crystalline spectrum of color across the lawn.

Travelers on the highway stopped in their tracks, many of them leaving their wagons and their chariots and rushing toward the house. The carpenters, who had risen early, to continue with the headquarters expansion, stopped their work to heed what Master Lucifer was doing. Warrior angels emerged from the house, and lined up proudly behind Lord Son of the Morning, to hear what he had to say.

"This looks different than his regular routine," Michael noted. "He is up to something!"

Never could they have anticipated just how bold Lucifer would be! Throwing his arms wide, he began to call to the masses who were thronging up from the valley.

"This is a great day, children. Come! Come! Hear what I have to say!"

The citizens were entranced, thrilled just to look upon his glory. As a body, they joined him.

"Your Master Lucifer has had a revelation!" he cried.

The citizens were amazed. "Tell us, Lucifer! Tell us!"

At this, Son of the Morning bowed his head, his face nearly penitent. For a moment, the archangels wondered if he might have come to his senses, at last.

But, his revelation was not so self-effacing.

"I feel I am not worthy of what has been shown me," he called out, his voice cracking.

How humble he looked! The onlookers were astonished.

"No, no, Your Imminence!" they cried out. "You deserve the highest gifts!"

Lucifer looked fondly on his worshippers. "Very well, then. I shall tell you! I trust you will not think me mad, but the revelation seemed almost to come from my own heart, so clear was it to me!"

"Speak, Lord!" they cried.

"It has been revealed to me that…I shall ascend…to the throne room! I shall be seated beside...the Almighty!"

The congregation was confounded. Many looked confused, disappointed, and turned away, heads bowed as though their hearts had been crushed. "How can he speak so?" they murmured. "We thought he was so noble, so trustworthy!"

Those who stayed to hear more, called out, "You shall sit beside the Almighty? How can this be? Only the Son has that position!"

But Lucifer's rationale was well-considered. "Have I not been placed in charge of the Father's New Creation? Have I not been given the darling of his heart?"

Those who had not already turned and walked away from this madness were amazed at his reasoning. Yes, it was true. He had been given oversight of the Father's pet project. Perhaps he was onto something.

Anger flashed through Lucifer's eyes, as he watched those who departed. But then he looked more fondly than ever upon those who stayed. "You are blessed, to put faith in your master!" he commended them. "Perhaps, yes, perhaps I shall rise even higher, still!"

Higher still? they wondered. What could be higher than to be equal to the Son?

The four archangels had meant to keep a low profile, but Michael, his face red as his flaming hair, could not bear another word. Flaring with indignation, he suddenly took out across the field, heading directly toward the crowd and "Master Lucifer."

Gabriel called out to him. "Be careful, Michael! This is no time for confrontation!"

Lucifer quickly spotted Michael's brash move. Thinking to turn it to his own benefit, he announced, "Ah, here is one of my captains! He will testify to the glory of our plans! Michael, come, speak!"

Michael was running now, straight through the crowd toward the veranda. His fist was raised, his eyes were bulging. "You would exalt your throne above all the angels of God?" he cried. "Who do you think you are, Lucifer? Do you think to rise above the clouds, to be like the Most High?"

Lucifer, however, did not retort. In typical fashion, he folded his arms and looked down on Michael as though he, and not himself, were mad. "Temper, temper, my friend!" he said, clucking his tongue. "You should not speak ill-advisedly. Are you choosing to turn against your old teacher?"

Michael was stunned, ready to fight, but finding no resistance.

Lucifer studied him sadly. "Oh, poor Michael. You always were a bit hasty. But, I am longsuffering. Do not disappoint me, my child."

Child! The sound hissed through Michael's

heart like a firebrand.

Enraged, he turned about and stormed back toward the pasture.

Reaching the other archangels, he spat, "It is time, comrades! Let's go!"

As a unit, they mounted their steeds. Gabriel followed Uriel and Raphael, who headed like lightning streaks up the highway. Michael pulled taut on his horse's reins, causing the animal to rear back, head high and froth flying from its mouth. Raising a fist in the air, the rider gave Lucifer a warning look which was wasted on the proud orator.

Michael gritted his teeth and took off to join his companions, the voice of Lucifer still audible across the growing distance. "Children of God," he was crying, "choose this day whom you will serve! If you choose Michael and his rebels, begone from me! If you choose the legions of the Morning Son, step this way!"

CHAPTER 17

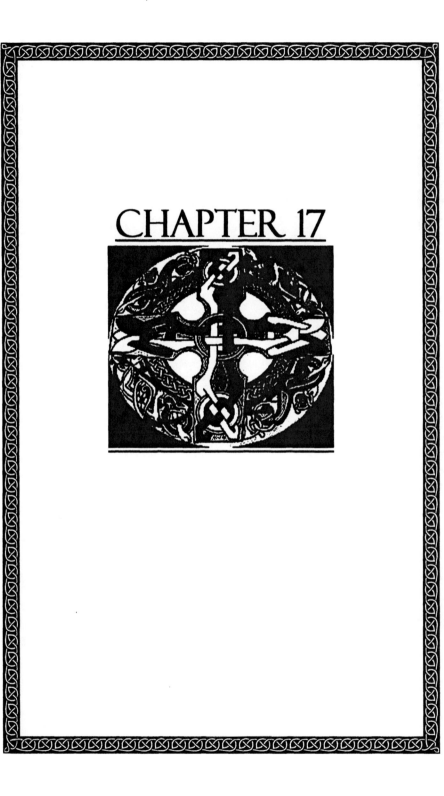

p the green valley, past the Tree of Life, following the shining ribbon called the River of Life, rode the four horsemen. Hearts pounding, knuckles white, they urged their mounts to greater and greater speed.

Ahead rose the steep cliffs whose tops were lost in the mists of the third tier of heaven, and it was at the base of those cliffs that they tethered their horses.

They had never known real fear before this day, though they had known sorrow. So weighty were both upon them that it was difficult to find the strength for flight. Michael, ever the leader, was the first to unfurl his mighty wings and push skyward. The others caught up with him quickly, but none of them moved with their usual grace.

Gabriel's body felt heavy. Never before had it taken exertion to elevate himself. His wings had carried him effortlessly upward, forward, downward, any way he cared to go. Now, he had to think through everything, as though the responsibility of the universe were crushing in upon him.

He could see the same effort on his comrades' faces. None of them was wholly well. A mysterious manifestation marred their spirits, and their wills. A villainous treason had invaded their domain, the entire realm of heaven.

Nothing would ever be the same again.

Gabriel remembered the first time he had flown up this cliffside. That day, he had only to think on the Father, what he might be like, how he might speak, how he would look, and suddenly his wings had grown. Those marvelous appendages had never failed him. They were as much a part of his being as his arms, toes, eyes. But, they represented so much more, something which only nearness to the Almighty could inspire.

Suddenly an idea posed itself: perhaps, if he were to dwell, right now, on the Father, his wings would regain their strength. Lately, Lucifer and his designs had dominated his mind. It was time to let that go.

Just as soon as he did so, he shot up, up, up, until he was lost to view in the mists above. His comrades, still struggling to keep aloft, called out to him.

"Let go!" Gabriel cried out. "Think of the Father…think of the Son!"

Only moments later, they all stood together on the green plain that led to the City Celeste. In the distance were the pearly gates, the spires and towers of the gleaming capital.

As soon as they laid eyes on it, their hearts were filled with joy.

But, just as quickly, they remembered why they were here, and they felt some of the heaviness return.

"How can we tell him?" Gabriel wept. "How can we tell the Son that darkness may overcome the light?"

Having passed the Crystal Sea, and wended down the streets of gold, they knew that, all too soon, they would approach the throne room. As they worried over what they would say, and how dreadful it was to bear the first bad tidings of all eternity, their footsteps were slower, their wings heavier.

They could just make out the glorious stairway that led toward the sacred chamber, rising above the forestland. They recalled the happy faces and cheerful greetings they had received from the angels who formed the banisters. How, now, could they enter that realm of purest light with a sad message?

Gabriel stopped in the pathway, and fell to his knees. "I cannot go on!" he cried. "I rose on wings of strength by thinking of the Father. Now, when I think of him, I can only imagine the great sadness I am about to bring to his loving heart!"

Michael and the others sat down in the pathway alongside him. They, too, had no spirit for their mission.

The four of them gave way to open weeping, loud and lusty. Tears poured down their faces and splashed upon the gleaming ground. For the first time in all timeless eternity, tears dampened the soil of heaven.

Would it never end, this awful sadness? Could light ever distill the darkness of their souls?

As they sat upon the ground, their arms entwined about one another, rocking back and forth while their brawny shoulders shook with grief, a soft sound managed to catch their attention.

Looking about, they heard it again.

"Archangels of the Almighty," it came, "where is your joy?"

At last, Gabriel spotted the source of the voice. Leaning against a tree, resting on the green grass, was the most lovely of heaven's inhabitants.

"The Son!" Gabriel cried. "It is the Son, comrades! See?"

He did not dare to point with his finger, but soon enough the others saw him, too. Instantly, they all bowed before him, pressing their faces to the ground.

The Son had not come with any entourage of attendants. His white horse was with him, and stood placidly by, munching on dewy grass.

He stood up and walked over to the angels, bent down and bade them join him.

The four comrades were weak-kneed as they followed him, and were grateful to sit down again, beside Him.

"It is a good day for a ride," he said. "Where are your horses?"

Michael managed to reply, "We left them at the border. We barely made it up the cliffs, and we have wings!"

The Son smiled, and nodded in the direction of a little green swale through which a stream ran. "It appears they had no trouble," he said.

Sure enough, there were their own horses, enjoying the pastures of the Lord's Mountain!

Had the angels forgotten that these steeds had only recently flown through the universe?

"Perhaps they are not heartsick, as you appear to be. Their spirits are light, for they do not worry," the Prince of Heaven said.

Gabriel choked back tears. How innocent was the Son! If he had any idea what they had been through, what they had seen, he would surely be heartsick, too.

And, now, were they supposed to tell him? Were they supposed to bring this perfect one the first awful tidings ever told?

"What is it, Gabriel?" the Son asked. "Why the long face?"

"Oh, Master!" he replied. "Must I tell you?"

The Son did not answer, only looking on his

servant with tender eyes.

"It is Lucifer," Michael intervened. "There is trouble down below, Your Highness."

The four of them braced for some awful calamity, such as they had witnessed the day the Father pulled back the curtain in the throne room and spoke of *choice*. Surely the very voicing of this wicked truth could rend heaven asunder.

But, there was no quake, no shaking of the mountains. Heaven was still and peaceful, just as always.

The angels cringed, looking about for some tardy consequence. But, nothing happened. The Son only nodded his head.

"Did you think I would not know?" he asked. "I created Lucifer."

Gabriel jolted. "Oh, certainly, Sir. You created everything. But not THIS Lucifer. Not the Evil One he has become. You could not have created HIM!"

The Son replied mildly, "Do you think you are not all capable of such a change? Haven't you seen that there are others who are willingly joining him?"

Uriel was inflamed. "How can this be? From where can Evil arise, since the Creator is Good?"

The Son stood up and brushed grass from his robe. "My Father calls it the *Mystery of Iniquity*. Evil is not created; it is chosen. And this choice is a simple thing, really, when you think about it. The choice between Good and Evil is simply the choice to love or not to love the Father, a choice which all of us have, dear friends."

Again, the angels braced themselves. The first time they had heard of choice, the foundations of heaven had rocked, the hilltops shuddered.

While none of that happened, Gabriel's heart raced. The Son was walking toward his horse, and Gabriel stood up. "Master!" he cried. "Do not leave! We would never follow Lucifer! We have made our choice!"

The Son turned and looked at them all, a smile stretching his face. "I know that, as well. I do not fear for your souls."

The four angels thought these words quite odd. Raphael sought an explanation. "You are concerned for Lucifer's soul?"

To their astonishment, tears welled in the Son's eyes. "I love Lucifer," he said. "I am his Creator."

At this, he took a deep breath and brightened. "Come, friends. Get your horses. Let's ride!"

As they galloped over hills and streams, through forests and glades, the black sorrow lifted. Gabriel would never forget this ride, the day he raced with the Son of God.

Such a wonderful laugh the Son had! It was deep and hearty, and filled them all with joy.

But, this respite could not last forever. As they neared the foot of the Lord's Mountain, the Son grew somber.

"It is time for me to go home," he said. "The Father and I have much to discuss."

Gabriel shifted in his saddle, yearning to hold him back.

"And what about us?" he dared to ask. "What do we do now?"

The Son did not give a hasty reply to this grave question.

"Hold onto the gifts you have been given," he said at last. "Michael, always wear your breastplate of iron; Raphael, be ready with the cup of healing; Uriel, do not withhold the flaming sword."

Then, to Gabriel, "You are God's Hero, my friend. And you are his trumpeter. Use your horn to rally the troops of God."

This last order sent a chill to all their hearts. Uriel could not miss the chance to ask the biggest question of all. "Sir," he said, "does this mean there will be war?"

The Son did not reply directly, but, as he turned away, spurring his horse toward the mountain, he commanded, "When you return home, grab your weapons!"

CHAPTER 18

hen the four horsemen returned to the second valley, their hearts were a conflict of emotion. Fear and trepidation were barely overcome by a sense of determination and courage. They knew the Son was with them, that the Spirit of God was their strength, though they could not see them. Still, there was no precedent for what they were about to face, no history to map the way or to predict the outcome.

They had just left the borders of the third tier of heaven, and were traveling down the highway that followed the River of Life, when they saw an odd phenomenon on the horizon. In the distance, above the region of Lucifer's headquarters, a flashing aurora of colors filled the sky. At the same time, a peculiar sound of chanting met their ears, borne up the valley on the midday breeze.

"What is going on?" Uriel marveled. "Is this Lucifer's doing?"

The horsemen nudged their mounts to a gallop and soon they were running swiftly down the road.

As they went, they came upon citizens who were running toward the head of the valley and the border they had just crossed. Many of them had packs of belongings on their backs, some were hauling household goods in wagons, some were holding hands with companions and glancing over their shoulders in fright.

Michael stopped the first group of refugees and demanded to know the meaning of their flight.

"It is Lucifer," they told him. "His pride portends no good for this valley!"

"Madness," another cried, as he fled past, his pack bouncing on his back. "Madness and wickedness!"

The chanting in the distance was growing louder, the kaleidoscope of flashing lights more brilliant. The riders continued on, until they could make out something strange coming toward them.

At first, it appeared like a dark mass moving up the highway, but then they could see that it was a group of beings, hundreds and hundreds of them, tramping up the road.

The archangels sorely wished they had their armor. Their hands tightened nervously on the horses' reins, wishing instead for their swords.

Still, the horde came on.

"Spread your wings!" Michael commanded his comrades. "Line up across the road!"

Instantly, they complied, Gabriel and Michael in the center, with Uriel and Raphael on the ends, to create at least a visual line of defense. Their unfurled wings spread as wide as possible, their horses stamping and snorting, they made an impressive sight.

Then, Gabriel had an idea. Grasping his silver trumpet from his saddle horn, he lifted it to his lips and blew dramatically, a few loud notes of warning. Michael looked at him with approval, then threw his own head back and filled his lungs. "Halt! Come no further!" he cried in his deepest voice.

At this, the oncoming multitude slowed down. Michael, taking courage from this, called out even more loudly, "We command you in the name of the Son, stand still!"

At this statement, Raphael looked a little askance. "Don't overstep yourself," he muttered.

But, Uriel, lifting his chin, said, "Well, we do have the Son's endorsement!"

Gabriel laughed softly, Baraq shifting from one hoof to another. "Whatever. It seems to be working," he said. "Look, they have stopped dead still!"

Michael clucked his tongue and his horse moved forward. The others, following suit, kept aside of him, an awesome wall of brawn and feathered might moving down the highway.

By the time they reached the crowd, many of whom had fallen to their knees in fear, they found that they were no threat. Though many of them were armed, they appeared to have no desire to fight.

As Gabriel surveyed them, he turned to Michael. "I recognize these characters," he said. "Look, there are some of the warriors and carpenters from Lucifer's house!"

Indeed, the mix included many of the angels who had been residing at the headquarters.

"What brings you this way?" Michael called out. "What is going on?"

One of the warriors emerged from the midst of the crowd and approached the four, his head lowered and his sword sheathed. Dressed from head to toe in bronze armor, he placed a fist on his chest in salute, and introduced himself. "My name is Fanuel, chief of the infantry. I honor you, Captain Michael, as Lord Commander. I do not bow the knee to Lucifer!"

Following behind him came another, this one dressed in mail and leading a fine chestnut stallion. He, likewise, kept his head down and saluted Michael. "I am Uzziel," he said, "chief of the cavalry. I shall never bow to Lucifer! I am at your command!"

In groups, warriors came forward, all anxious to clear themselves of any implication with Lucifer. The carpenters and citizens who had come out with them proclaimed their innocence as well, gaining courage from their leaders, until their chorus was a roar of proclamation.

"We shall not bow to Lucifer!" they cried. "We shall serve Michael and the Son!"

Gabriel was taken aback. "So," he said, "it has come to this, has it? Lucifer has finally set himself squarely against Immanuel!"

"Yes, Captain Gabriel," Fanuel reported. "His pride is beyond reckoning!"

Uzziel added, "You should have heard him just today! As he addressed the crowd, he drew the battle lines then and there. We had no choice but to make a choice!"

Gabriel's skin crawled. There it was again, that word. *Choice!* The choice "to love or not to love The Father" was being played out before their eyes.

Michael saluted the two warriors and hailed the crowd that had separated themselves from Lucifer's wicked scheme. Then, leaning down from his horse, he said to Fanuel and Uzziel, "We must go and retrieve our armor. Take command of our little army, and guard them 'til we return."

Fanuel pounded his fist against his chest, again. "Yes, sir!" he replied.

Uzziel, likewise, saluted, then stepped closer. "You will find your armor is safe enough," he said. "We put a couple of good guards in charge of it."

CHAPTER 19

s the four horsemen raced down the highway, the strange aurora above Lucifer's headquarters pulsated, as though it were a living thing. In fact, the colors seemed to take the shape of an enormous winged creature, a lionish, reptilian beast, the nature of which they did not recognize.

Arising toward the phantasm, amidst fiery, flashing light, were huge billows of smoke. And the chanting grew louder, accompanied, now, by rhythmic, metallic beats.

The archangels could only imagine what any of this portended. Forcing their way beyond fear of the unknown, they dashed straight past a line of guards at the border of the yard and headed toward the house. The instant they entered the smoky arena, they saw that the metallic percussion that mixed with the chant came from a hundred anvils, on which Lucifer's workers forged weapons of black iron.

The citizens and warriors who busied themselves in Lucifer's service did not take much notice of their arrival. Much to the archangels' amazement, when they did notice, they stood at attention, saluting them as they raced toward the house.

If Son of the Morning saw them, he did not let on, busy himself with vociferous self-adulation.

Back and forth he strutted on his veranda, waving his arms and proclaiming, "Son of the Morning, highest thought of the Father, who can deny my pre-eminence? Master of a New Order, I shall ascend to the Holy Mountain, I shall lift up my throne above the throne of the Most High!"

Michael led his comrades around to the grove where they had hidden the day Gabriel returned from his celestial journey. There they tethered their horses and squatted on the ground, waiting, listening to the blasphemous diatribe.

"He has utterly lost his mind!" Raphael gasped. "The creature makes himself greater than the Creator!"

Gabriel followed the dazzling movements of his old mentor, the lights of whose robe reflected the fire of the hundred forges into the air above. "Look!" he cried. "This is the source of the strange beast in the sky!"

As they peered above, they could see that every time Lucifer spread his arms, the winged beast raised its wings, every time he threw back his head, the beast appeared to roar. So much did the lights resemble reality, it was hard to believe that a gigantic and terrifying double of Lucifer did not hover above them.

"It looks like a dragon!" Gabriel marveled.

Michael shook his head. "It is only an illusion," he said. "Don't be afraid, fellows!"

But, Michael's face belied his confidence. The others could see he was as frightened as they.

Now, Lucifer's harangue was more daring, as he repeated what must have been his theme since they had left this place. "Join me, comrades!" he was crying. "Do not let the old mysteries enslave you any longer! Grasp for yourselves the hidden wisdom which the Father and the Son have kept to themselves!"

Hidden wisdom?

"What is he talking about?" Uriel asked. "The Father has given us nothing but love and light, from our first breaths!"

Michael sneered. "Lucifer knows nothing which would benefit anyone. He is a self-deluded fool, thinking he has the power of God in his own hands!"

Gabriel clenched his fists. "He is a liar!" he spat. "The Father of Lies!"

Michael clapped Gabriel on the back. "Hold that thought," he said. "We had better make our move, now, while he is still in his wild trance!"

Gabriel agreed, but shot a nervous glance skyward. Michael nudged him. "It is not real!" he insisted. "It is part of his charade! Come, now! Let's be going!"

As a unit, the four headed toward a set of

stairs that entered the veranda out of view, and they slipped through a side door into the house.

Scurrying about were workers and carpenters, who had styled themselves as soldiers. Awkward in their newly forged armor, they stood at attention the moment they saw the archangels.

"Captain Michael!" they greeted, saluting him as though he were their commander. "We have been waiting for you. Master Lucifer said you would tell us what to do."

Michael tensed, scarcely believing Lucifer's presumption. Gabriel leaned close and whispered in his ear, "The fool could not believe we would really leave him! He expected us to repent and come crawling back!"

"Apparently!" Michael said with a shrug. As he stared at the waiting troops, he wanted to cry out, *The best thing you can do is abandon this farce, before there is no turning back!* But he thought it best not to tip his hand so easily.

Instead, he raised his chin and demanded to know where the archangels' armor was.

"It is still in the hall, Captain," one of the workers replied. "No one has touched it."

Giving an abrupt nod, Michael, with his comrades, headed for the rack where the weapons had last been seen. As soon as they got there, they discovered how it was that their armor had been kept safe. Two enormous mastiffs stood before it,

"Join me, comrades!" he was crying. "Do not let the old mysteries enslave you any longer!"

fangs bared and eyes glowing.

Gabriel smiled. "So, these are the guards which Uzziel mentioned!"

"Very good!" Michael laughed.

As soon as he spoke, the animals sat down in meek submission, ears relaxed and mouths closed. Gingerly, the archangels stepped forward and patted them on the heads.

"Fine fellows," Raphael said, soothing them with his kind voice.

Michael was the first to reach for his sword. He had not held it since the day he and his comrades had been summoned to the inner sanctum of the throne room. Eyes wide, he lifted it from the peg and fondled the glistening hilt.

One by one, the others followed suit, then, leaning their swords against the wall, they began to don the suits of armor that hung there.

As for Gabriel, this was a most awesome moment. He had not actually held his sword since the day he was created, having left it on the green hill when Lucifer led him away to meet the others. As he lifted it from off the rack, he was not content to merely stroke the hilt, but actually cradled the weapon in his arms, studying the shining beauty with gleaming eyes.

Michael nudged Uriel. "Look at God's Hero," he teased. "He dreams of performing great feats."

Raphael chuckled, giving his leggings an extra tug. "Enough, Gabriel!" he said with a laugh. "You will get to know that sword better than you ever cared to, if Lucifer doesn't repent."

Repent...Now, there was an odd word, and one never used before in all the annals of heaven.

Gabriel's face twitched and he set the sword down. As he donned his own armor - which included leggings of brass, a breast plate and helmet of silver - his heart thundered. What were the chances, he wondered, that Lucifer might change his mind? What hope in heaven that he might recant?

The four were now fully garbed and, one by one, they grabbed their shields of radiant bronze from off the wall. They were just admiring one another's daunting magnificence when the mastiffs at their feet suddenly stood up, poised and rigid.

The noisy hallway, full of bustling warriors, had fallen quiet, and someone cried out, "His Highness, Prince Lucifer!"

The tramping of two of Lucifer's closest henchmen preceded the arrival of the proud traitor. As he entered the hallway, Gabriel was stunned to see that his face seemed darker, the glow of his beautiful countenance strangely dim. Perhaps smoke from the forges outside had left soot upon it, he thought.

Yet, curiously, his robe was more brilliant,

its gems virtually throbbing with light.

The great dogs, lips curled back, revealed white teeth, but when Lucifer looked their way, they slunk back, whimpering.

The dark prince paid them no mind, his own teeth bared in a broad smile, as he stepped in front of his two guards.

"Michael!" he cried, his arms spread wide. "Welcome home! Gabriel, Uriel, Raphael...my dear friends! I knew you could not desert me!"

Wheeling about, he addressed the two henchmen. "Did I not tell you?" he boasted. "My captains could not betray their old teacher!" Then, turning again to the archangels, he introduced his companions. "This is Belial," he said, "and Beelzebub. You will come to appreciate their loyalty, my friends. If I did not have you, they would be my generals. As it is, let them be your warlords."

Michael turned up his nose as he looked over the strapping guards. Gabriel hoped he would not make some imprudent retort. To his relief, Michael stifled his seething emotions, hiding a clenched fist behind his back.

Lucifer, meanwhile, circled the red-haired angel, admiring his glorious armor.

"You do our cause great justice," he said. "All of you, my friends, are warriors of the highest order, and you certainly look the part!"

Gabriel bit his tongue, and glared at the floor. How he longed to be away from this wretched place!

"Well," Lucifer said, satisfied with the inspection, "our foolish rebels had better think again, before they face the likes of you!" Then, rubbing his chin, "By the way, did you see any of the traitors who fled this place?"

Michael's face reddened. Clearing his throat, he replied, "We did, sir. Several bands, actually."

Son of the Morning seemed to detect hesitance in Michael's tone.

"Yes," Lucifer said, his voice smooth as silk. "I imagine you did."

For an uneasy space, there was silence.

"So," Lucifer, said, fingering the gems on his sleeve, "you have not told me why you left, what you did, where you went." His gaze penetrated Michael's heart. "Shall you tell me now?"

Gabriel was astonished that his red-haired friend was able to keep his composure. His reply, to Gabriel's mind, was utterly brilliant.

Head high, Michael stared unflinching at his challenger, and even managed to smile. There was not a hint of duplicity in his words, as he said, "Actually, we were gathering an army, of the very rebels you just mentioned."

Lucifer's body grew taut, his eyes narrowed. The warriors up and down the hall murmured amongst themselves.

But Michael did not waver, his eyes holding Lucifer's with steadfast confidence.

Suddenly, Lucifer seemed to relax. What could possibly account for Michael's unruffled demeanor if he had not won back the rebels to the cause? Why, of course! That must be it!

Throwing his head back, Lucifer let go a hearty laugh. "Oh, my friend," he chuckled, "you had me going there! You almost had me thinking you were gathering a force to come against me!"

Belial and Beelzebub absorbed this nervously, but then, they too gave way to fitful laughter.

Gabriel, Uriel and Raphael looked at one another in amazement, shifting in their armor and clearing their throats.

As for Michael, his expression did not change, giving no hint of the coup he had just pulled off.

Lucifer, whose pride would not admit of any treachery to himself, indulged in hilarity, before he finally got a grip on his emotions and resumed his dignity.

Looking his supposed generals up and down, once more, he confirmed his approval. But, as his eyes traveled to the inscriptions on their shields, *Glory to the Lord*, they narrowed again.

"So," he said, "you will be going, now?"

Michael nodded. "Yes, sir, to look in on our new troops."

"Very well," Lucifer sighed, turning for the door. Then calling over his shoulder, "But do something about those shields. *Glory to Lucifer* has a nice ring."

CHAPTER 20

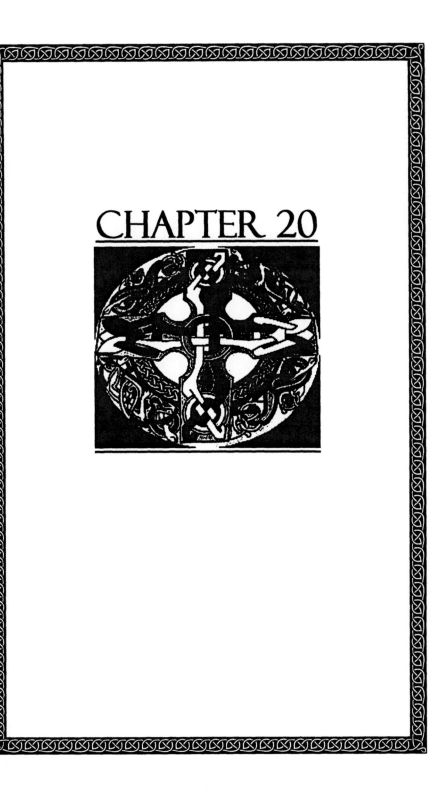

zziel and Fanuel, the rebel warriors who had valiantly led the refugees out from Lucifer's seductive fortress, warmed themselves over a forge in the middle of Camp Michael.

While the archangels had been getting their armor from the house of wickedness, these stalwart fellows had been organizing their band of untrained warriors and citizen soldiers into the semblance of a battle-ready contingent. The first order of duty had been to arrange a camp, which they had named for their commander.

Of course, it would not be easy to drill amateur troops quickly enough for war, but they were determined to go beyond what seemed possible. Beginning by dividing the troops into platoons, and naming sergeants over each, they had left them to set up the camp.

Fanuel and Uzziel were grateful for the warmth of the forge. A strange chill had settled over the valley, the first time in heavenly history that the temperature had been less than mild. The chill had arrived hand-in-hand with another phenomenon, an odd darkness that had descended on the valley like a blanket.

Both of these peculiar changes seemed to have arisen from the vicinity of Lucifer's domain, and the pall seemed heaviest over his house. At first, observers thought the darkness was merely a result of smoke from Lucifer's forges. They knew, now, that it was more than that. They knew it was a phantasm of Evil.

Against this bleak background, the winged reflection which was associated with Lucifer and his spangled robe, danced, dipped and dove, taunting all who looked upon it.

Fanuel and Uzziel kept their gazes averted from the phantom, feeling in their bones that it was not healthy to pay it any mind.

The four archangels, likewise, avoided direct witness of the eerie specter as they headed up the valley. Although they had tried to convince themselves that it was merely a charade, it seemed to have a spirit of its own, or to at least be a true reflection of Lucifer's heart, as well as his garment.

In fact, as they had taken leave of the house, Gabriel was certain he had heard Lucifer call it by name. *Power*, he had dubbed it.

As they rode away, Gabriel told Michael what he had heard, but the captain looked skeptical. "It is true!" Gabriel insisted. "I heard him call it by name, as though it were…a living being!"

Raphael and Uriel were not so doubtful as their leader. "After all," Uriel said, "we all have our horses. Perhaps this Power is his companion, one that will do his bidding, just as our animals do ours."

Michael shook his head. "That is wild speculation!" he cried. "You are letting your imaginations run away with you."

But, Gabriel noticed, Michael did not look over his shoulder at the flashing apparition, which actually seemed to watch their departure from high in the sky.

A chill went up Gabriel's spine as he nudged his horse to a faster clip. He took peculiar solace in the fact that the two great dogs who had guarded their weapons ran beside them.

Gorgeous animals, they were, one tawny-gold with soft black ears and face, the other gray-black with a white splotch on his massive chest. Gabriel would ask Uzziel what their names were. For now, he called the one Barley and the other Smoke. It seemed they had attached themselves to the angelic company, and he was sure they would continue to serve them well.

The four horsemen could scarcely believe their eyes, as they came upon the neatly arranged Camp Michael, the lights of which beckoned them a short distance from the road. The members of the encampment greeted the arrival of their commanders with a hearty shout.

Speeding through the cheering company, the

archangels reached down from their mounts, clapping their soldiers' uplifted hands and bestowing their approval. Gabriel, his heart swelling with pride, punched the air with his fist, rooting for his troops.

Such a welcome sight were this bunch of amateurs. Michael looked over his shoulder and gave Gabriel a wink, as though to say, "They aren't much, but we will shape them up."

It flashed through Gabriel's mind, as he smiled back, that the archangels were, in truth, amateurs themselves. How could it be that anyone present knew more about war than any others?

Yet, he realized that some of them had been created for the art of war, and others were less naturally endowed. Dreadful as the prospect of violence was, he felt in his bones that he had an untried talent for it, and that his three companions were like himself.

He watched Michael's reception with admiration. Everyone knew the red-head was the top leader. He had already proven his cleverness and his bravery in dealing with Lucifer. He had a hot temper, which could pose problems along the way; but, Gabriel figured he was aware of it, and that he would master it without undue damage.

As for Gabriel, himself, he was not sure of what his natural abilities consisted. Sometimes he considered his name a cumbersome enigma:

God's Hero. What could that mean? What challenges lay ahead that would call for heroism? And what sacrifices would that heroism demand of him?

At the center of the camp was the large forge where, even now, sturdy weapons were being crafted. Inventories of spears, swords, shields, helmets and other gear lay in tidy piles about the grounds, and soldiers were lined up to receive their supplies.

Fanuel and Uzziel saluted Michael and his captains as they swung into the supply zone.

"Greetings, Commander!" they hailed him.

Michael dismounted, landing like a seasoned equestrian on easy feet. Pounding his right fist to his breastplate, he returned their salute. "Good day, gentlemen!" he said. "It looks as though you expect a battle!"

Fanuel nodded, his face stretched in an eager smile. "So we do!" he replied.

Gabriel and the others also dismounted, Barley and Smoke keeping pace as they joined the inner circle.

"And none too soon," Uzziel noted. "The darkness grows thicker down yonder."

They all turned to look in the direction of Lucifer's headquarters. The sound of pounding hammers and rhythmic chant reached them even at this distance.

And above the dingy horizon, where the forges of evil fabricated weapons of rebellion, the dancing griffin dipped and swayed.

"Eerie creature, isn't it?" Fanuel said. "What do you make of it, Captain?"

Michael's face twitched ever so slightly, but he made no reply. Gabriel stepped forward and answered for him.

"Son of the Morning calls it *Power*," he said.

"It seems to be growing with the darkness," Uzziel observed.

Michael's eyes narrowed. "He would have done better to call it *Pride*," he scoffed.

Raphael made his own observation. "I think there is little difference, " he said. "Lucifer's pride bolsters his power and his power spurs his pride. They are a wicked knot, those two."

CHAPTER 21

abriel nestled between the roots of a large tree, some distance from the forge. The orange glow of the fire filled the otherwise dark sky with a tentative light, but he sat in the tree's shadow, in a space bleaker than he had ever known.

Barley and Smoke were curled up on either side of him, giving him some solace in this gloomy hour. Uzziel had never named the dogs, as they had come to him "out of nowhere," he said, and just in time to stand guard over the archangels' weapons. So Gabriel's choice of names was fine by him.

Gabriel ran his hand over Barley's smooth ears, wondering at how such a strong animal could be so soft to the touch. All of the Father's creatures were marvelously made, he considered, and each one had its purpose and its place.

Providence was all around, he realized. These fine dogs were just one example of the Father's caring. Gabriel comforted himself that God had always provided, had always known what he would need, before he knew, himself.

He thought back to the way words had come to him, how understanding had grown as he required it; he remembered how Baraq had entered his life, quietly unassuming, a necessary companion on his celestial journey; he remembered how the map of the universe had appeared in his saddle bag, showing him where he was and where to go; he remembered finding his trumpet slung casually on his saddle horn, a badge of his calling. And, of course, he remembered his sword and shield - two items in which he took rightful pride, but for which he had, so far, had no need.

God knew that he *would* have need of them. This was a certainty which he did not question.

But when would the first challenge come? When would he lift sword to strike, or shield to defend? It would surely not be long. The eerie darkness was growing thicker by the heartbeat.

Until a few moments ago, Gabriel had been stationed on the brow of the hill just outside camp, overlooking the highway. Michael had finally sent Raphael to replace him, but what he had witnessed as he stood watch had unnerved him.

All along the minor roads and byways of the valley, streams of light were flowing toward the highway. At first, he was not certain of what he saw, but gradually it became clear that the lights were flaming torches and glowing lanterns, carried by pedestrians leaving the villages and towns of the area. Amidst the streams of walkers were vehicles, some horse drawn wagons, and others fancy chariots, like the one Gabriel had ridden in the day he met the Son at the Tree of Life.

Whatever the means of travel, the citizens were converging on the highway, at which point the merging streams divided, the greater part heading toward the border of the higher level of heaven, the rest toward Lucifer's headquarters.

Arising with the sound of the tramping feet and the rolling wheels toward the place where Gabriel had been stationed, were sounds of dissension and quarreling. Never before had he seen the residents of heaven argue or fight. The few times that Michael had confronted Lucifer were the closest to discord anyone had ever witnessed.

Apparently the members of the many households in the kingdom were in conflict, bickering over whom they should follow: Lucifer or Michael, Lucifer or...the Son. Pushing and shoving, some of them actually came to blows before they parted.

Those who raced toward the upper border warned those who would join Lucifer that their fate was surely sealed in some unthinkable perdition, while the rebels accused them of being spineless, mindless slaves to a dictatorial God.

Gabriel pressed even closer against the tree, put his hands over his ears and buried his forehead against his updrawn knees. The sound of Lucifer's chanting minions, the blast of hammer on anvil near and far, the sounds of haranguing and squabbling from the valley floor - it was all too much for him.

The hovering blanket of smoke from Lucifer's forges had overtaken Camp Michael, whose own forges were not so large or numerous. Gabriel lifted his eyes and gazed north toward the City Celeste, whose bright light still managed to penetrate the darkness. How long would it be before even its glory was overwhelmed by Lucifer's suffocating pride?

Suddenly, his ruminations were interrupted by a booming voice, crying out across the valley: "My friends! It is not too late! Leave this wickedness and return to the heart of your Father! Do not be overcome by the scheming of a maniac!"

It was Michael, calling after the citizens who were making their way toward Lucifer's encampment. Arms and wings spread wide, he stood upon the brow of the hill where Gabriel had earlier kept watch, and Raphael was by his side, like a sentinel. The fires of his own forges lit his back, casting him in silhouette for those below.

"Repent, and return to the love of the Almighty!" he cried. "What has our Father ever done but good for us?"

Gabriel left the tree and stood a distance away, watching the reaction of those who heard

Michael's plea. He could see that some of them had second thoughts, that they considered turning back. Then, there were others who tugged at them, scorning their reticence.

All at once, a great billowing sound issued on the southern wind, like shuddering sails in a howling storm. A dreadful screech filled the air and, suddenly, the awful griffin, the dazzling serpent of Lucifer, came sweeping up the valley.

Drawing the atmosphere into a gale, a mighty wind attended it, whipping the tree tops, stirring the waters of the River of Life into a roiling froth that splashed in powerful waves over the riverbanks. The roar of a storm, never before heard in God's perfect heaven, split the air, causing Gabriel's hair to stand on end.

Barley and Smoke whimpered up at him and pressed in close to his legs. He bent down to stroke their massive heads, but had no words of comfort, his own heart bleak as the eerie sky.

There was no light now, except the glow of torches along the highway, fires in forges, and the unwelcome sparks cast from the glaring jewels of the spangled griffin. Its eyes, also, were illuminated, a sinister, mocking green, pierced through with tinges of yellow hate.

It had grown to two or three times the size it had been when the archangels left the headquarters. When it reached the point where

Michael stood below, its wings spanned the valley from river to hill, and the awful aura of its glistening scales cast spasmodic gleams across the camp.

Michael, not to be cowed, stretched his own wings wider, displaying the radiant whiteness that was a reflection of his heart. Throwing his head back, he raised his sword and flashed it in the air. "Woe to you, O Wicked One!" he cried.

The griffin hovered overhead, its long neck arched indignantly, its snaking tail whipping the sky. The talons of its huge feet could have picked off a hundred soldiers with one flick, but it made no move, only glaring down at Michael with such hatred as could melt iron.

Its fantastic, scaly wings, ribbed with gigantic stays of bone, shuddered back and forth, keeping its enormous body aloft with little effort, but creating a vacuum that nearly pulled the archangels off their feet.

"Woe to you, Power of Lucifer!" Michael called again, waving his sword and holding his shield before him. "Return to your house of Evil!"

From the depths of the griffin's throat issued a horrifying hiss, a sound such as had never been imagined in heaven's history. Spitting, tongue darting from its mouth like that of a lizard, the great Power studied its opponent.

This one is not worthy of my attention! it seemed to conclude, as it reared back and swiftly let fly two streaks of flame from its nostrils. Lowering its head, it belched an inferno, singeing the ground at Michael's feet.

Gabriel rushed forward, joining Raphael, and from somewhere behind came Uriel, his own sword drawn, and it with a fiery glow. Together the archangels stood, side by side, their unfurled wings forming a white wall, their heads uplifted and their weapons straining for the sky.

The griffin now began to move from side to side, ascending a bit, then circling, staring down on them as if to see what they were made of.

To the rear of the archangels, the hosts of Fanuel and Uzziel scrambled to arrange themselves in ordered lines, spanning the brow of the hill in waves, one behind the other. Below, along the highway, the citizens stood stone still, mesmerized by what they witnessed.

Again, Power let fly a wailing screech, which made everyone jump. The citizens, sensing that there was no time to flee, rushed back off the highway, seeking shelter behind rocks and trees.

Then, in one deft flex, Power poised its neck like a bow, its great muzzle taking aim on the roadside. With a trumpeting snort, it released a torrent of flame that set the vegetation afire where the citizens hid out, forcing them into the open, where they fled screaming.

Michael itched for vengeance, and his comrades with him, when another sound, even more menacing than Power's blast, ascended from Lucifer's camp. It was the cry of war, the shout of the denizens of Evil, accompanied by the rush of ten-thousand feet, up, up the valley floor.

Gabriel held his sword aloft, hand tingling, heart throbbing, as the griffin hoisted itself skyward and fanned its way back toward its master's palace.

In the black, smoky distance, could be seen the minions of the Morning Son, spears and swords gleaming in the light of a thousand torches.

Hither marched the legions of Lucifer. The War in Heaven had commenced.

CHAPTER 22

nce it began, matters transpired in such rapid succession, it was impossible to keep track of them. It appeared this battle would be cloaked in a shroud of smoky darkness, light piercing it only with the flash of torches.

While Gabriel and his comrades had prepared for the coming assault, the ranks at both ends of the valley had been swelling. News of Lucifer's rebellion had been spreading for a long while, since he had first begun to give his diatribes on the veranda of his house. Folks throughout all the levels of heaven had been compelled to choose whom they would serve. The nature of the conflict permitted no middle ground, no compromise. And, since Lucifer would abide no delay, everyone had, by now, taken a side.

Whether or not they were warriors, all the heavenly citizens were compelled to lend their assistance to the endeavor as they saw fit. Not only did warrior angels take up arms, but so did carpenters, builders, masons, and the many who were built for endurance. Artists, cooks, gardeners, writers, teachers, accountants, and all the other angels of all the less physically demanding professions aided the efforts as best they could.

As the minions of Lucifer marched north

toward them, Gabriel left his comrades and flew over the landscape to survey Michael's army. He was astonished, and pleased, to see how enormous it had grown. Besides ranks of foot soldiers, angels who owned horses had joined the force, making for a splendid cavalry; with them were charioteers in shining vehicles, their own horses harnessed in bronze.

Thousands upon thousands filled the hillside, armed and ready. As Gabriel passed overhead, he saluted them and they, in turn, hailed him as one of their chief commanders.

Seeing the magnificent steeds, done up in their gear, he thought of Baraq. He remembered that he had left him tethered to the big tree where he, himself, had sat with the two dogs. "Good boy!" he called to him, as he flew to his side. He stroked his long neck lovingly, untied him and hopped into the saddle. "Let's go!"

Turning him about, he headed back to the command post and brought his mount alongside his fellow generals. His sword was sheathed, but his trumpet was at the ready, hanging on his saddle horn.

Michael looked at him approvingly. "Are you ready to play that thing?" he asked with an edgy laugh.

"You know I am!" Gabriel eagerly replied.

"Then, you had better begin now!" Michael

...this battle would be cloaked in a shroud of smoky darkness, light piercing it only with the flash of torches.

commanded. "Give notice to all our forces. The time is at hand!"

Gabriel pounded his fist into his breastplate, whipped his horn from the saddle, and wheeled his horse about. Speeding up the hill, he skirted the ranks of all the troops, blowing on his trumpet.

"Prepare! Prepare!" he called between lusty blasts. "The forces of Evil approach!"

Because Camp Michael was set on a hill, the archangels had a clear view of the enemy's approach. Michael thought it best to hold his ground and not advance until Lucifer's forces were within bowshot.

Tension filled the ranks as they watched and listened to the advancing horde. The sound of thousands of tramping feet, the clatter of chariots and stamping horses, the rustle of shields and staves, all made for an intimidating din.

"Hold your ground!" Gabriel called out to his warriors, as he rode back and forth along the army border.

Behind a protective row of chariots were the horsemen and infantry, a haphazard lot to be sure, though enthusiasm for their cause more than compensated for their mismatched weaponry and lack of uniform. The faces of the charioteers, the bowmen and shield bearers with their long spears, were bright, not only with anticipation, but with an inner glow that emanated divine confidence.

Gabriel's heart swelled at the sight. As he returned downhill, he threw his head back and called at the top of his lungs, "Hold steady, Sons of Light! Listen for Michael's call."

Suddenly, a host of flaming arrows filled the sky, arcing up the valley and landing on the grassy hillside. A wall of flame sprang quickly to life, rushing up the slope toward Michael's station.

In an instant, water wagons sped forward from the area of Fanuel's forges; rolling back and forth across the hill, they released fans of cooling liquid over the ground. Michael's horse stomped nervously, as flames neared his hooves, but within moments the blaze was extinguished.

Michael raised his fist in the air and brought it down quickly. At this sign, Gabriel trumpeted again and the Forces of Light rushed forward to meet the Darkness in the vale of conflict.

Thick blackness covered the entire valley, the fracas commencing to the glow of torches. Wheel to wheel, hand to hand, the clash ensued, the lead transferring from side to side and back again, so quickly, there was no accounting for it.

Gabriel had returned his trumpet to the saddle horn, wielding a sword, instead. The choking smoke stung his eyes, but did not blind him to the horrors all about.

He would never forget the first time he saw

Michael commanded, "Give notice to all our forces. The time is at hand!"

an angel wounded. It came only seconds into the first confrontation, and it was a dark angel who fell. As he did so, a flicker of light, dull, sullied and fleeting, escaped his closing eyes. Arising through the dank air, it dissipated, accompanied by an eerie, maniacal shriek, which seemed to travel down the valley toward Lucifer's camp.

All around, troops were falling, both good and evil. Gabriel had never heard the word *death*. It had never been spoken in the heavenlies, nor even imagined. But, angels were dying, all about.

There was an awful, stunning difference in the way the Sons of Light departed and the way Lucifer's minions met their demise. While a grotesque chorus of shrieks rose from the evil doomed, Gabriel's comrades met a more peaceful transition. The light of their departing souls was full blown as it left their bodies, and joined with a cloud of others that formed a canopy above the army, aiding in the efforts of their comrades.

Still, it was a shocking and horrifying thing to witness anyone's downfall. Gabriel's stomach churned and he steeled himself against the fear of wounding. What would he do if one of his three companions were to fall? How would he manage to go on? He did not want to know.

Pressing in close to Michael, he held the center of the foursome as they kept up an even advance. It was not until he heard an agonized whimper, that he realized Smoke and Barley were nearby.

"Oh, Father, no!" Gabriel cried, as he spied Barley in a heap upon the dark ground. "He's been hit!"

Why it would occur to Raphael to help this poor creature, when many of his own troops had already fallen, they would never know. Perhaps it was because the animals had been swept up in this fray through no choice or doing of their own, that his sympathies were more easily pricked. But Michael, Uriel and Gabriel watched in amazement as Raphael pulled out from the elite corps and headed to Barley's side.

Leaping down from his horse, he knelt beside the dog and drew the golden cup from his sleeve, the one which symbolized his calling.

"Here, comrade," he said, cradling the dog's head in his lap. With a swift movement, he pulled an arrow from the animal's side and, after removing the silver lid from the cup's rim, quickly poured a thick, aromatic ointment into the wound.

In a few moments, the dog groaned and struggled to its feet, gaining strength by the second, astonishing all who looked on.

A mighty shout of exultation went up from the ranks of Michael's army. "Raphael! Raphael!" they chanted, over and over, applauding the Healing Angel. As Raphael held his chalice aloft,

Barley standing proudly by his side, the leaders of the contingents came forward with flasks, ready to be filled with the unending supply from Raphael's cup.

Quickly, the flasks were passed among the troops, and they poured the soothing balm into wounds and even upon the bodies of their departed comrades. The injured were healed, the spirits of the fallen reunited with their bodies, and a thrill of wonder and joy passed through the ranks that nothing could contain.

Shouts of praise rang forth, swelling over the valley and up to the borders of the highest level of heaven, where, Gabriel figured, they must surely meet the ears of God himself.

Raphael's three comrades looked on through tears of amazement, as their army was infused with unstoppable zeal. Confidence swelled through the ranks, a strange new light glowing from faces and bodies, filling the hillside and the sky above with radiance.

Gabriel shielded his eyes from the utter glare of it, then looked back down the valley toward Lucifer's troops. Stunned, they had stopped in their tracks, gawking at the brightness.

Gabriel took a deep breath, his face stretched in a smile.

"What can defeat us, now?" he said, leaning toward Michael. "It seems we are invincible."

Michael observed all that transpired with a bit more caution. "Not so hasty, my friend," he said. "This war in only beginning. I feel it in my bones."

CHAPTER 23

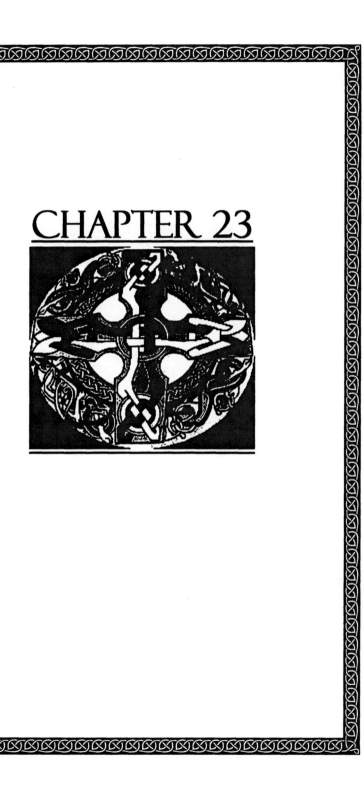

abriel's name for Michael's forces, *Sons of Light*, took on its full meaning when they attained their glowing brightness. From the moment they knew life was eternal, that they did not need to fear the wounds of the enemy, they shone like stars.

Advancing in full fury against Lucifer's stunned hosts, they chased them all the way back down the valley, until they were within sight of the enemy's headquarters. They sent the soldiers of the Dark Side to their doom by the dozens and the hundreds, causing the air to be filled with the eerie wail of the vanquished, the vacuous howl of lost souls.

It was not until they were about to advance on the headquarters, itself, that they were brought up short by a frightening vision. Suspended above the house was the griffin, Power, with his steaming nostrils and his fiery tongue. His colossal tail was wrapped about his body, and within its coils, held close to his body, were the thousands of fallen enemies, apparently alive!

The dragon seemed to be cradling them, as though nursing them back to full strength, and as they came to, regaining themselves, he swooped over the highway, depositing them on the ground. Full of vigor, they raced toward the Sons of Light, more ready than ever to wreak vengeance.

A bizarre lot they were, not the same glorious beings who had so recently deviated from the path of Good. These, while the same persons, were hideous to look upon, hunched, scaly, fanged. They did not so much run as amble, ape-like, using their knuckles to propel them, as well as their enlarged feet.

They were of every imaginable description, some horned, some toad-like, some like crouching lizards, a ghastly horror to behold. However they had come to life, they were translated, no longer merely fallen angels, but the fully possessed of Lucifer who would henceforth be called *demons*.

Gabriel shifted anxiously in Baraq's saddle. "Michael, how can this be?" he marveled, his face etched with revulsion. "They have no healing angel, such as we have; they have no flasks of curative ointment!"

Michael shook his head. "I have no idea!" he replied, surveying the advancing legions with wide eyes. "Sound retreat, Gabriel!"

The trumpeter had just lifted his horn to his lips and blown enough notes that his troops knew to turn and run, when, all of a sudden, two large angels of Lucifer confronted him on their mounts, long spears drawn and ready to charge. They were still some distance away when he realized he would have to face them head on, or be chased hopelessly to his demise. The certainty of eternal life did not quell all fear.

He had no spear, but he brandished his sword furiously and, pressing himself close to Baraq's back, thrust his heels into the horse's sides and rushed forward. As he charged, he recognized his opponents as the two generals of Lucifer, whom the Evil Lord had introduced to the archangels the day they went to retrieve their armor. Belial and Beelzebub he had called them.

Apparently among the mightiest of God's hosts, these two had been a grand prize for Lucifer's side. They were an intimidating sight, their strong physiques done up in lavish bronze gear. It was clear that they had not yet been wounded in this fray. They were not part of the ghoulish contingent whom Power had revived. Gabriel cringed to think what they might look like, had they been of that macabre force.

"Lord, preserve me!" he cried, as he galloped headlong between their horses. Whipping his sword from side to side, he managed to deflect their lances and to send Belial crashing to the ground in a metallic thunder. Beelzebub flew past him and turned about, his horse's hooves swirling a cloud of dust into the smoky air.

As Belial groaned upon the ground, Baraq straddled him, allowing Gabriel to thrust the point of his sword into his throat, where his helmet and collar parted. A gurgling sound rattled upward with his departing gasp, and as Gabriel spun backward, the escaping spirit of Belial glared down upon him with such hatred as could have crippled a weaker soul.

Meanwhile, from behind came Beelzebub, his horse's pounding hooves sending a tremor through the ground. Baraq danced away from Belial's limp body and, lowering his head, barreled toward Beelzebub's mount as though he were, himself, a warrior. Gabriel gripped tight the hilt of his sword and dashed straight toward Beelzebub's lance, intent on breaking it in two. He could hear the enemy's breath, as the great, dark angel panted toward him.

"Father, protect me!" Gabriel cried again, as he came alongside the advancing foe and brought his sword crashing down at right angles across his spear. With a mighty crack, the lance split, so close to Beelzebub's body it nearly ripped into his breastplate.

"Aiyee!" cried Beelzebub, his horse skidding to a halt and turning again to charge.

At this point, Gabriel became aware that these clashes between himself and the enemy generals had captured the focus of everyone within sight. The battle nearby had come to a virtual standstill, as both the forces of Good and Evil watched the titanic struggle.

A dreadful wailing ascended into the sky from the Dark Side, upon seeing that Belial had fallen. Clanging their shields and spears upon the ground, they created a terrible din, both of mourning and revenge.

"Beelzebub! Beelzebub!" they chanted, as their warlord wheeled about to face the archangel.

One of the dark legionnaires tossed the general a sword, seeing that his lance was broken, and Beelzebub did not miss a beat in his advance.

Meeting face to face, the two contenders whipped and dashed their swords against one another, first one and then the other gaining the upper hand. At one point, their arms were intertwined, their faces so close they could smell each other's breath.

"It is not too late, Beelzebub!" Gabriel groaned through clenched teeth. "The Father will surely forgive you, if you repent of this wickedness!"

Beelzebub spit violently, his green eyes boring into Gabriel's as if to melt them. "Which is worse, one tyrant, or another?" he hissed. "At least I had the courage to act on my own! How will you ever know what you might have been, Lord Gabriel, had you half my nerve?"

Tears stung Gabriel's eyes. "Take no pride in choice alone!" he cried. "It is *what* you choose that matters!"

With this, he managed to extricate his arm from the enemy's, and, pulling back, got an expedient angle. With a powerful lunge, he buried his sword into Beelzebub's breastplate, through metal, through flesh, through bone.

With a look of actual surprise, Beelzebub clutched at his chest and fell backward, crashing to the ground in a disgraceful heap. Gabriel leaped from his horse, braced a foot against Beelzebub's breastplate, jerked his sword free, and waved it triumphantly in the air.

The shrieking wails of the enemy forces knew no boundary, as they rushed forward to wreak vengeance on the Sons of Light. But, at the witness of Gabriel's victory, the side of Good shone more brightly than ever, and the enemy could scarcely advance for the blinding glare.

Slashing and tramping, the godly forces overran their assailants, and, for the moment, the tide of battle turned in Michael's favor.

The leading archangel rushed to Gabriel's side. "Well done, friend!" Michael shouted, leaning down from his horse to meet Gabriel's hand in a hearty clap. "We see, now, how worthy you are of your name!"

But God's Hero was not ready to rest on these achievements. His eye had been caught by movement along the parapets of Lucifer's house.

The Lord of Darkness had been watching all

that transpired, and Gabriel could see, by the way he turned on his heel and left the roof in a flash of his robe, that he was not ready to settle for defeat.

Overhead, the griffin paused, eying his master and the field below. Some of the dark troops, seeing the wicked creature, seemed to read his gaze and saluted him. Then, as if following some unspoken command, they rushed toward the bodies of their fallen generals and dragged them off across the dank ground.

"Where are they going?" Gabriel asked, directing Michael's attention to their retreat. "Where are they taking the bodies?"

Michael observed the odd activity with a gimlet eye, then studied the hovering dragon.

"I don't know," he replied. "But I think it would be wise to find out."

CHAPTER 24

abriel rested on the brow of the hill where he and his three comrades had watched this war's beginning. Behind him, by the forge and beneath the trees that dotted Michael's encampment, wounded Sons of Light received the ministrations of Raphael's healing balm, or recouped from their warring in small huddles.

Below, in the valley, the battle still raged, the upper hand traded back and forth between the sides. Though the soldiers of Good blazed forth in glory, their light impervious to the dark assailants, they did not always overcome the Evil that opposed them. For every dark angel that fell, another took his place, more often than not a previously fallen comrade who was now one of the diabolical imps revived by some mysterious alchemy within Lucifer's control.

Michael had chosen a handful of his cleverest warriors to go off on a mission of espionage. "Discover, by whatever means necessary, where they are taking their dead," he commanded. "Do not return until you can tell us how they are reviving them."

The spies had been gone too long, it seemed to Gabriel. He kept watching for them upon the highway, though it was possible they had taken a more circuitous route to and from Lucifer's camp, to avoid detection.

With a heavy heart, he cast his eyes toward the borders of the highest level of heaven. What might the Son be doing, right now? he wondered. Was he aware of the atrocities being played out beneath his peaceful abode? What could he be doing that was more important than intervening to stop all of this?

Gabriel remembered the Son's parting words, when he had left them to take on this conflict. "The Father and I have much to discuss," he had said.

Had they been "discussing" all this while?

Gabriel knew the Father's heart was full of the New Creation which he was about to undertake. But, could those plans and preparations be so important that they overshadowed what went on in his own beloved heaven?

The archangel remembered Lucifer's infatuation with that same cause, how he had sat, day after day, hunched over the confounding map in his dining room, watching the swirling mass that represented the uncreated realm move and grow across the dark blue paper.

Not for the last time, Gabriel marveled over the mystery of Lucifer, himself. Just who was he, and what was his story?

Gabriel's pensive ruminations were

interrupted, when, as he scanned the road below, he suddenly made out a little entourage of angels heading north. By the looks of them, they were not the returning spies. Nor were they warrior material. Their robes of the purest white, they could not have been involved in any warfare to this point. Composed of youthful characters, both masculine and feminine, the group rode in a long wagon led by two rather slow donkeys. The driver, also dressed in white, glanced nervously about, and called out to the donkeys with high-pitched urgency. "Get along now, Grey-bones!" he called. "Move, Long-ears! We must not linger here!"

Gabriel's heart lurched. He could scarcely believe his eyes. It was the music teacher of Kinnowr and his students!

Leaping to his feet, he called Baraq to him and jumped into the saddle. Racing downhill, he cried, "Hail, musicians! Hail!"

The wagon jolted to a stop and the donkeys looked blankly at the archangel. The teacher and his students gawked at the dazzling being, speechless to find him here.

"Good evening, friend," Gabriel said, bringing Baraq to a stamping halt beside the wagon. "What brings you to this dangerous place?"

The little fellow tugged at his wispy beard and bowed. He was about to answer, when Gabriel said, "You know, I never inquired as to your name. I am Gabriel, one of the four generals of this army." He stretched out his right hand toward the Sons of Light arrayed across the valley. "And you are.."

"Uh, Natsach, sir. I...we knew you were a mighty lord, but we had no idea..."

"I was only an emissary when you met me," Gabriel said. "Neither had I any idea of what lay ahead for all of us."

The music teacher nodded sadly. "What is to become of us?" he asked weakly. "Do you think the Father has forgotten we exist?"

Gabriel was pricked at the heart to hear his own doubts so plainly voiced. "Of course not! He has not forgotten."

Natsach, whose name Gabriel recognized as meaning *choir master*, looked anything but masterful at the moment. In fact, it was difficult for Gabriel to imagine him doing anything but teaching students in the little hamlet where he had found him.

Gabriel got off his horse and stepped up to the wagon, looking at the sad little character with sympathetic eyes. "You should not be here, you know. What brings you to this awful valley?" he asked again.

Natsach sat back and tried to sound strong. "We had to come!" he declared. "There will be many such as ourselves, arriving from all the planets of music, in the next while. We all felt it at once, the urge to come. The Father's New Creation must be very close to dawning!"

Gabriel thought again of the map in Lucifer's parlor. "Quite possibly so," he agreed. "So, you have come to join the celebration?"

It was hard to think in terms of celebrations and merriment, under the circumstances. The words caught in Gabriel's throat.

"It was your command that we prepare," Natsach reminded him. "We have been doing so, all along. Now we yearn to blend our voices and our music with the choirs of the highest level of heaven…if they will have us."

Gabriel smiled wanly. "They will welcome you!" he insisted. Then, looking sorrowfully to the south, he said, "As for me, I must remain here, to see this through. Such was the Son's command to me and my comrades."

Natsach was amazed, his students whispering among themselves in wonder. "You have seen the Son?" the choir master marveled. "Oh, what is he like? Is he as beautiful as they say?"

Gabriel's skin stood in gooseflesh at the memory of the Father's Beloved. "Beyond description," he said. "No one can ever be the same, after meeting him." The archangel bowed his head. "His breath is the life of us all."

Natsach looked sadly toward the border of the third level of heaven. "Yes...I know this. And, it is true, then...He has not forgotten us."

For a moment, the sounds of war dimmed, thoughts of the Son crowding out all darkness for the little gathering. At last, however, Natsach grew bewildered. "How could Lucifer do what he has done?" he asked. "Considering that he was once the closest of all heavenly beings to the Son..."

Gabriel jolted at these words. "What did you say?" he gasped. "What do you know about Lucifer? Tell me!"

Natsach was taken aback, fearful of Gabriel's vehement reaction. Shaking his head, he stared in wonder at the enigmatic warrior. "Can it be that you know nothing of this matter?" he marveled. "How long have you known Lucifer?"

Gabriel was chagrined. "It must have occurred to you that I have but recently come to be," he admitted. "When I visited you on Kinnowr, I knew little of the universe, the planets...didn't you guess?"

Natsach tried to hide a knowing grin. "I did suspect as much," he said. "But, I did not feel it appropriate to question you."

Gabriel lifted his chin. "In this, I am not ashamed," he said. "But, there is much I wish to understand. Lucifer was my mentor, from the moment I took breath. Very quickly, however, my comrades and I came to feel there was something amiss, that Lucifer was not so good as he seemed."

Natsach lowered his eyes.

"So, tell me!" Gabriel said. "What is the great mystery kept from us all this time? Who is this Son of the Morning, really?"

Natsach picked his words carefully. "Once upon a time, very long ago, I was summoned to visit the highest level of heaven. I was called there to receive my credentials as a teacher of music."

"Yes, do go on!" Gabriel urged him.

"I saw Lucifer come out from the inner sanctum that day. He was serving as the covering angel for the Son's entourage as he went on some outing. I could not see the Son, but I will never forget Lucifer's glory. Matchless...beyond description! Why, even his robe..."

Gabriel stopped him there. "Yes, I know the robe," he said with a bite. "It is his greatest show of power."

Natsach did not comprehend the full implication of Gabriel's words, but continued, "You see, sir, Lucifer was the anointed cherub, *The Angel Who Covers*, they called him. He was the closest of all the Lord's companions, his best and dearest friend. And he must have been his first created being, for his name means..."

"*Son of the Morning*," Gabriel said.

The little musician watched in fear as the warrior clenched and unclenched his fists, his nostrils flaring with burning anger.

At last, the little fellow glanced at his cargo and peeped, "Well, sir, if it is just as well with you, I think we must be going."

Gabriel stepped away from the wagon and saluted the smaller angel. "Take word to those above, will you? Tell them how things are going here."

Natsach brightened at the order. "It will be my duty and my honor!" he declared.

"I owe you much, Natsach," Gabriel said. "You have made many things clear to me. If there is anything I can do for you, let me know."

Natsach flicked his whip at the donkeys' backs and clicked his tongue. "Just win this war!" he said. "If Lucifer has his way, life itself will be eternal death!"

CHAPTER 25

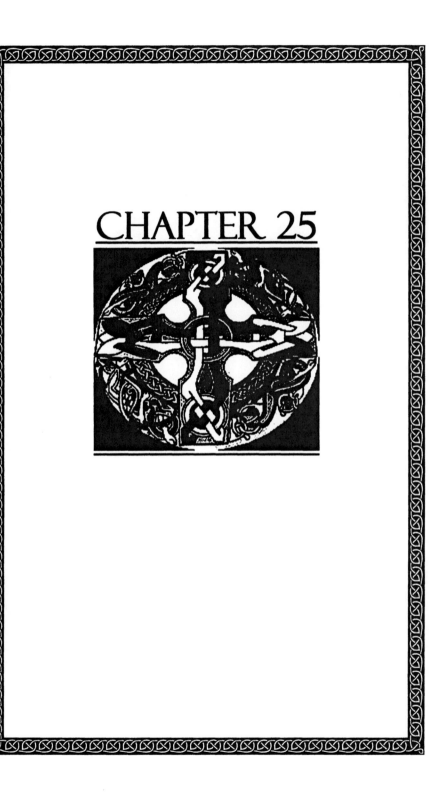

s Gabriel watched Natsach hurry up the highway, his parting statement haunted him. "Life itself will be eternal death ... death ... death."

Something in those words stirred his heart strangely, not only because they were the most foreboding ever spoken, but because they seemed to contain the key to a mystery.

"Life itself ... eternal death," Gabriel whispered. And then, it dawned on him. "That's it!" he cried. "That is how they are doing it!"

He jumped into Baraq's saddle and fled down the highway, away from Camp Michael and skirting the thickest part of the battle. Following the River of Life, he headed for the great tree that spanned the flood, knowing Lucifer's secret.

What could have revived the fallen enemy but the leaves of the Tree of Life, the leaves whose healing tincture could revive anything, the perpetual preserver of all life!

And how would the gift of life be used by the Wicked One except to strengthen forever the corrupted souls of his fallen demons?

"Preserved unto eternal folly!" Gabriel cried, as he raced down the road.

This explained the decrepit nature of their

resuscitated bodies. The fallen angels of the Dark Side were not restored to the beauty of their original nature, but were revealed in all their inner ugliness - bent, hunched, groveling, menacing, ravening. Such they had become, through their own choices, and such they were now configured for all eternity to come.

Indeed, Gabriel thought, for these desperate ones, life was eternal death.

But, Gabriel could not let them take control of the Tree of Life! It must be rescued from their lustful powers, or life would never be the same in God's heaven.

Speeding on, he passed others like Natsach and his companions, newly arrived from the musical realms. It must be that the Father's plan was about to be undertaken. Would the New Creation be born on the very brink of heaven's demise?

This, too, must be prevented. The New Creation would surely go forward, but heaven must be reclaimed!

Suddenly, he saw, amid the new arrivals, the group of spies whom Michael had sent out. Rushing up the road, lashing their horses to faster and faster pace, they were about to pass Gabriel without recognizing him.

"Halt!" he cried, catching them before they went by. "Have you a message for Michael?"

"Oh, Lord Gabriel!" they cried. "You will never believe what we found!"

Gabriel nodded. "I think I will," he said. "The Tree of Life, right? That is where they are taking the bodies?"

Amazed at his insight, they were about to question how he had guessed, but he had no time for explanations. "Go!" he commanded. "Tell Michael what you saw! And send Uriel to help me. We will need the aid of his flaming sword!"

Conditions at the Tree of Life, when Gabriel arrived, were worse than he could have imagined. Dark angels, some who were still in their prime and others who had been revitalized to exist in deformity, hauled corpses of their fallen comrades toward the river. Self-appointed medics anointed the wounds of the dead and washed the bodies in a potion of curative leaves and fruit mixed with water from the life-sustaining river.

One after another, after another, the dead arose, greeted by the applause and cheers of their rescuers.

A morbid, grisly sight it was, to see the once robust beings come to. Though they were alive, they looked at their scaly hands and legs, felt their own hideous faces with crabbed fingers, and they groaned ambivalently, relieved to be conscious, but shamed to be such as they were.

Gabriel darted off the side of the road and hid behind a bush, observing the procedure with a churning stomach. What could he do against so many? Yet, he must do something! The Tree of Life was being systematically stripped of its leaves and its fruit by the greedy scavengers. The small animals and birds who dwelled among the branches had been forced to seek the highest points, where they clung in desperate fear to the tiniest limbs, chittering and cawing helplessly as their home was ravaged.

Suddenly, despite the odds, Gabriel felt compelled to take a stand. "Are you ready, boy?" he asked, bending close to Baraq's ear. "You must be nimble, now. Let's go!"

Baraq reared back, infused with passion for the challenge, then lunged forward, directly into the thickest gathering of the unprepared enemy. There were presently no corpses on the field, all having been revived, when Gabriel came sweeping into their midst.

Lashing at them with his sword, he cried out, "Shall you die twice, you Wretched Ones? Who will revive you then?"

Ruthless, unstoppable, Gabriel ripped at Lucifer's ghouls, parting many of them from their bodies for the second time. The shrieks and howls of these damned creatures was far more grotesque than when they died the first time. *The Second*

Lashing at them with his sword, he cried out,
"Shall you die twice, you Wretched Ones?"

Death, history would call it, sent these spirits into a disembodied state from which they would forever be desperate to free themselves. It would not be their lot to enjoy even the crippled forms of which they had been dispossessed, but they would, instead, forever seek to dwell within others, ravenously coveting bodies, any bodies, to inhabit.

Gabriel could not foresee all of this. He was bent on only one thing: the reclaiming of the Tree of Life.

His stunned victims scrambled for weapons with which to defend themselves, as Gabriel carved a wide path between them and the tree. Though they rallied, they could not overcome his advances before he was joined by Michael, Raphael and Uriel, who had raced out from camp.

"Fine work!" Michael shouted over the screams of the doomed, his own sword slicing a bloody pathway before him. "You have not left much for us to do!"

Gabriel was unspeakably grateful for his comrades' arrival. "We must set Uriel nearest the tree!" he cried, as he fended off encroaching challengers. "Only his sword can keep them at bay for long!"

Michael, catching Uriel's eye, gave him a nod, and the angel whose name meant *God's Fire* turned his mount aside and raced toward the quaking tree. There he leaped to the ground and held his sword aloft, swinging it like a warning beacon, back and forth.

Nowhere, among all the weaponry of all the warriors of Light and Dark, was there another sword like Uriel's. Radiant, vibrating, it hummed with sacred energy, capable of severing Good from Evil, Right from Wrong, Truth from Lies. The moment he planted himself between the roots of the tree, the desecration was over.

The instant the enemy perceived that their source of rehabilitation was out of grasp, they seemed to lose focus. Fearful, desperate, they turned to flee, Michael, Gabriel and Raphael close on their heels.

All the way to Lucifer's headquarters they were chased, and as Gabriel came within sight of the horrid parapets, he knew the end was near.

Whatever happened next would determine heaven's future, for Good or for Evil.

CHAPTER 26

ord spread quickly across the stage of battle, among both sides, of Gabriel's heroic victory at the Tree of Life. As Uriel stayed behind to continue guarding the precious prize, the three other archangels raced across the fields, chasing the demon forces toward Lucifer's headquarters.

Gabriel wielded his sword with his right hand, and held his reins and trumpet aloft with his other, sounding the charge with long, persistent blasts that reached to the highest level of heaven.

From every corner of the war zone, focus shifted to the Dark Lord's citadel, final stronghold of Evil. The Sons of Light, their hopes and zeal bolstered by Gabriel's victory, made a clean sweep of the field, charging over the fallen enemy and making for the castle's looming walls.

Earlier, Gabriel had seen Son of the Morning as he paced to and fro atop his fortress. He had not been pleased when he saw the demise of his generals, Belial and Beelzebub, and just now he could be seen leaning over the parapets, his hands gripping the stone stanchions in dismay.

As Gabriel recalled the confrontation with the two head demons, he wondered what had become of them. They had died upon the field, but had they, too, been revived? If they had been,

Gabriel cared not to meet them in their diabolical state. Powerful as they were before dying, they would surely be intimidating devils.

He cleared his mind of such fears and kept pace with Michael, whose massive horse seemed never to tire.

And what of Michael? he wondered. While Raphael had fulfilled his role as healer, Uriel as the Fire of God, and even Gabriel himself was now rightly called God's Hero, Michael had yet to achieve his full potential. Raphael's chalice was the perpetual balm of Light, Uriel's sword the defender of Life, Gabriel's trumpet the messenger of Triumph. What of Michael's breastplate? Was there yet some challenge that would prove its mettle?

He figured so, and he figured they were about to meet it.

The forces of Good and Evil were head to head, now, hand to hand. At the base of Lucifer's headquarters, they faced off in the most vicious conflict yet chronicled.

As this activity played itself out, the archangels were already considering the final barricade to be leapt, the final endeavor to be waged. The headquarters of Lucifer must be taken!

They had not yet answered the question *How?*, when, in skirting the edifice, they discovered a storage area stockpiled with amazing war machines. Fanuel and Uzziel would have given anything to have such capabilities as these instruments represented. Enormous catapults, with huge boulders piled on wagons, were lined up in perfect order. Battering rams on mammoth wheels were prepared for some unannounced plan.

Gawking at the awesome creations, Michael made the obvious deduction: "Lucifer's madness knows no bounds! He intends to storm the City Celeste, and take the Holy Mountain, itself!"

Raphael pounded his saddle horn. "Not unless we permit it!" he spat.

Gabriel clapped the healer on the back. "Well said," he replied. "So, now we know what we must do!"

Michael sat up straight, a smile stretching his eager face. "How thoughtful of Lucifer to leave these machines for us! Raphael, go rally the troops to take control of this stockpile. Attack the fortress from the walls inward. As for Gabriel and myself, we will work from the inside out!"

No one knew the house of Lucifer better than the two Sons of Light who secretly invaded it. As the war raged outside, the troops of Fanuel and Uzziel rushing to take control of the war machines, Gabriel and Michael crept under cover of smoky darkness onto the veranda and entered the side door.

The house's interior was virtually undefended. A few skittering demons flitted to and fro in search of hiding places, so engrossed in their own self-protection that they did not notice the intruders. The sound of war was beyond the walls, somewhat muffled by stone and mortar.

The two archangels tiptoed down the hall, past the rack where their armor had once hung, and headed for a set of back stairs that led to the roof. Blackness filled every room, and Gabriel found his courage unexpectedly challenged.

There was some unseen evil here, perhaps the spirits of disembodied demons watching them, and causing Gabriel's hair to bristle.

They were just about to set foot on the bottom stair heading to the roof, when Gabriel grabbed hold of Michael's sleeve. He felt compelled to tell him what he had learned of Lucifer, as though the sharing of this secret should enter into the decision to go forward or retreat.

"Michael, I must have a word with you," he whispered. "There is something you should know."

Michael frowned. "Now? This is no time for conversation!"

Gabriel shook his head. "I think there will be no other time."

Michael leaned against the wall and crossed his arms impatiently.

"I have learned who Lucifer is," Gabriel began.

Michael sighed in exasperation. "What do you mean?" he grumbled. "We know who he is! He is the enemy of God Most High!"

"Of course," Gabriel agreed. "But he was once the Son's dearest friend. Do not ask me how I know this. I have no time to go into it. But, trust me. It is true!"

Michael was skeptical. "I think the strain of war has gotten to you," he sighed. "Lucifer could never have been that glorious."

Gabriel nodded. "So we presumed. But, we never really knew. No, Michael, there must be a long history to his jealousy. Lucifer goes back a long way."

When Michael was unconvinced, Gabriel reminded him, "What do you think *Son of the Morning* implies? He was the *first* of the Father's creatures!"

Michael tried to control his voice as he snarled, "So be it! What if this is true! Have you forgotten how far we have come? Do you, after all this time, still fall to defending Lucifer?"

Gabriel was stunned, Michael's old accusation sinking into his heart like a knife. Tears sprung to his eyes, as he declared his innocence. "How can you suggest such a thing? It is *you* I defend, Michael. Whatever comes of this foray, it will be your ultimate face off with the Evil Lord! I don't want you to underestimate him!"

This seemed to subdue the leading angel. With uncharacteristic meekness, he bowed his head. "Very well," he said. "I shall take your warning to heart."

CHAPTER 27

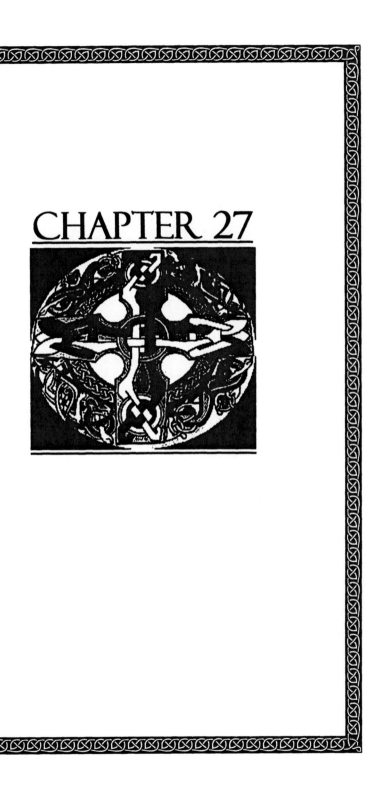

ogether, the two friends proceeded up the stairs, each step taken cautiously, ears strained for any suspicious sound, as the walls of the mansion reverberated to the first assault against it.

Fanuel and Uzziel had wasted no time in enlisting the war machines. Volley after volley of massive artillery pummeled the stronghold, causing the two invaders to grab at the stairwell to steady themselves.

At last, they reached the top tread and stopped, holding their breath, listening for any sound from the rooftop. Michael pressed his back against the wall and ever so slowly poked his head above the exit. Gabriel, scooting alongside him, did likewise, both of them barely peeking above the landing.

To the far corner of the front barricade, Lucifer stood, hanging over the parapet and watching the onslaught below. To the dismay of the two archangels, he was not alone. Behind him stood two massive warlords, done up in bronze, their blue-black skin oily between opalescent scales. From their heads sprouted curving horns, giving the aspect of grotesque rams, and their eyes were calculating pinpoints of wickedness, green and hate filled.

Gabriel slumped back and took a step down, his chest constricted with fear. Michael, joining him, deduced his thoughts. "Belial and Beelzebub," he whispered. "Am I right?"

"They can be none other!" Gabriel said. "I knew I was not done with those two!"

Perhaps it had been ill-advised of them to ascend inside a house which was under siege. When the next volley of the catapult careened into the building's façade, the stairwell shifted ominously. Losing their footing, Michael and Gabriel were thrown down, clattering upon the stairs in their armor.

Their surreptitious invasion was secret no more. Belial and Beelzebub snorted, rushed toward the stairwell and sniffed for intruders.

Michael struggled to his feet and lifted Gabriel with him.

"Ready?" he asked.

"Ready!" Gabriel replied.

In a bound, they were in the open air, their swords poised for contact.

Michael was confronted by Belial, Gabriel by his partner. To their astonishment, the demons were twice the size they had been in their first life, each a colossus of vile wickedness.

As for Lucifer, he had never borne a sword, and wore no armor. He apparently assumed he was above the need for such trappings. But, this was not to say he was defenseless.

As the fight proceeded, Michael and Gabriel showing astonishing dexterity and resilience, it looked as though Lucifer's generals might be taking the worst of it. In that moment, Gabriel caught a movement out of the corner of his eye. Lucifer was on the attack.

It was not with weapons of steel or iron that he lashed out. It was with a flourish of his arms, a flash of his spangled robe, and a cry of, "Come, Power! Overwhelm my enemies! Take what is yours for the taking!"

Suddenly, like a lightning bolt, Lucifer's griffin blazed across the sky. His enormous wings shadowed the entire valley, creating a storm with every rise and fall.

A screech of vengeance filled the air that must have been heard in the throne room, itself.

As though Michael, and Michael alone, were his target, he careened downward, barreling straight for the red-head. Even Belial and Beelzebub rushed aside, lest they be flattened by his descent.

Just as he came within inches of Michael's face, he stopped, his wings holding him in a strike position. To the archangel's horror, he reared back, took a monstrous breath, and let fly a streak of flame directly toward his chest.

Gabriel lifted a hand to shield his own face

from the stunning heat. But when he dared look again, he saw that Michael was still standing. His breastplate, which should have melted in the blast, was still solid.

In fact, the only change to Michael's armor was that the symbol upon that breastplate glowed radiantly.

Glory to the Lord! it declared.

Michael looked in amazement at his protective vest, and his eyes grew wide.

"Glory to the Lord!" Gabriel cried. "Who is like the Lord?"

Michael raised his fist in the air. "Glory to the Lord!" he also cried. "Come and get me, Power! My God is far more powerful than you!"

Lucifer glared at his griffin, shaking his robe and sending him aloft to strike again.

But, it did not matter how many times Power attacked, he was no match for Michael.

The sounds of assault on the building had tapered, the troops of both sides having stepped back to watch the rooftop spectacle.

"Michael! Michael!" the Sons of Light called out. "Who is like the Lord?"

And the Sons of Darkness set up a sparring chant: "Power! Power! Lucifer shall never fall!"

Raphael, not to be left out, rushed into the building and up the stairs. He would help Gabriel take on the two Dark Generals. Uriel, likewise, having established a guard about the Tree of Life, joined the fray.

Still, the Minions of Darkness would not relinquish their revolution. Back and forth the lead was traded, the war in full force again, while the four archangels contended above.

It was beginning to seem that the conflict would go on forever. Gabriel's grip weakened, only to grow strong again; he stumbled, only to rally, over and over.

Power swooped across the landscape, burning the mountains, destroying any beauty that was left. Would Lucifer, still strutting and posturing, see all of heaven destroyed, rather than give up his fight?

"Father, where are you?" Gabriel cried, lunging for the hundredth time at his opponents.

"Son of God, help us!" Michael prayed. "We cannot hold out forever!"

At that instant, something happened which would go down in the annals of heavenly history as the greatest of all events. Across the highlands to the north, such a blaze of white light flashed, that it split the darkness over the valley, cut through the smoke and dissipated the dank odors of war. Such a vivid brilliance blasted the landscape, that everyone fell back, shielding their eyes lest they go blind.

Even Power let go a screech of pain, turning

tail to the mountain and heading back to his master.

A rolling bank of white overswept the terrain, and gradually it could be seen that the cloud was composed entirely of Beings of Light, descending from the Holy Mountain. At their head, in the very forefront of the advancing throng, was the Son, riding upon his white horse, layers of golden crowns upon his head and a gleaming sword within his hand.

Gabriel cowered flat against the rooftop, shielding his eyes until they adjusted, somewhat, to the suffocating glare.

Gradually, the Sons of Light were able to bear the witness of the Son of God in all his glory. Was this what Lucifer had once covered, the awesome Light of God that was nearly too much for lesser angels to endure?

The beings who accompanied The Son were not an army. Gabriel recognized them as the seraphim who continually beheld the face of God, the holiest beings in heaven. They need not act in force, for they were so glorious, a mere look at them was enough to take the breath away.

They were *the train* that filled the temple, the hallowed entourage who forever praised their Lord. To think that Lucifer had once been mightier than they!

Like rolling thunder, the Son's voice was

heard, swelling over the valley. "How art thou fallen, O Lucifer, Son of the Morning! How art thou fallen who once attended the Son of God!"

The archangels managed to stand, as the Son descended toward Lucifer's domain. They watched in stunned silence as he lifted his sword, and, bringing it down swiftly, created a bolt of lightning that caught the dragon by the tail.

Flinging his arm upright, he caused Power to spin about like a whirlwind, a vacuum that lifted the Forces of Evil off the ground. Like leaves in a storm, they whirled and tumbled until they lit on the griffin's tail, caught in his scales like struggling mice.

Gabriel blinked his eyes, wondering if he imagined all this. But now, Lucifer, himself, was staggering on the rooftop, clinging to the parapet, resisting the pull of the cyclonic wind. His generals, likewise, fought the tug, but at last lost their footing and were swept up like so much chaff, into the coils of the griffin's appendage.

"O, Lucifer, Lucifer!" the Son cried. "You were sealed with perfection from your first breath. You were dear as my heart, until unrighteousness was found in you!"

At last, Lucifer lost his grip on the barricade and was spun into the air. Splayed against the dragon's back, he had not strength to lift a finger.

"Begone!" the Son called, dashing his

sword against the open sky. "Heaven shall no longer be your home!"

With this, the dragon and its horrid cargo were flung away, spinning, spinning, until only the flashing sparks from its bespangled hide could be seen, a kaleidoscope of departing color dissipating through the universe.

EPILOGUE

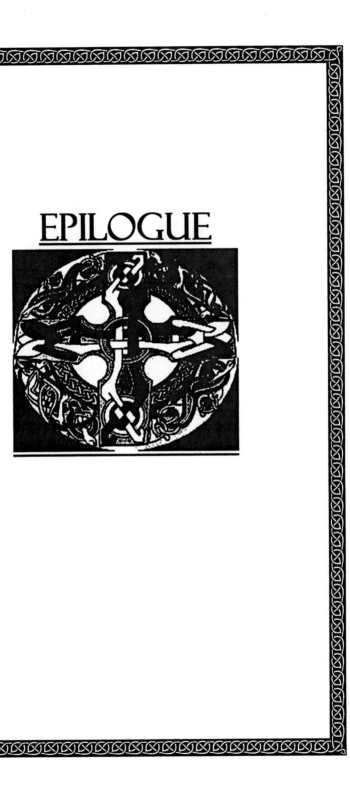

abriel, Michael, Raphael and Uriel walked through the rubble that had been Lucifer's headquarters, kicking at the broken stones. It had been many days since the war had ended, but it would be many more before heaven was restored to its previous glory.

Worker angels labored non-stop to clear out the ravages that conflict had left on the valley. In time, outward evidence of the rebellion would be obliterated from the scene.

But, the inward effects of Lucifer's sin would never be entirely wiped away. The innocence of the heavenly angels would never be quite so naive, the scars of Lucifer's revolt would never entirely disappear from their hearts.

This was not all bad. The realization that wickedness had once existed here made appreciation of God's goodness all the more profound. The memory of Lucifer's demise would forever be a testimony to God's righteous love.

Furthermore, the Sons of Light could rest in certainty that their peaceful realm would never again be threatened. The War in Heaven had demanded an accounting: who was on the Lord's side, and who was not. The choice had been made, once for all. Never again would they have to fear rebellion, for the Father of Rebellion had been cast out, taking a third of the angelic host with him.

Still, there were questions. Sometimes, the four archangels pondered them together, but today, as they wandered through the heap that had once been their own home, they were rather silent, each caught up in private rumination.

Upon their chests, four medals were hung, suspended by satin ribbons of royal purple. These medals had been given them by the Son, when the war was ended. He had invited them to his palace, where they were received with much celebration and much ceremony, as genuine heroes. Now, they awaited further orders. For, they sensed, their work for the Son had only just begun.

"Do you think Lucifer was utterly destroyed?" Gabriel broke the silence.

His companions had wondered this many times, themselves.

"I sincerely hope so," Michael replied. "But, whether or not he was, he has no power here."

As they crossed the point where the parlor had once stood, Gabriel's eyes were caught by the charred remains of the dining room table. Barley and Smoke, who were always at hand, sniffed the rubble and pawed curiously at the ash.

A vague notion came to Gabriel, and bending down, he lifted the table top, peering beneath.

Yes! There it was!

"Hold this for me, will you?" he said, leaning the broken top into Raphael's hands.

Getting on his knees, he scrounged in the rubble beneath, until he uncovered a long roll of paper. Barley sat down with a whimper, as his master pulled it out and dusted it off, exposing the dark blue parchment of the old map.

Raphael laid the table top on the stony floor and they all knelt there, as Gabriel unrolled the scroll. Together, they searched for the odd, swirling mass which had identified the embryonic beginnings of the New Creation.

"Here it is!" Gabriel cried. "See, it still moves and flashes!"

Uriel's eyes lit up with that inner fire which was uniquely his own. "It is more active than ever, don't you think?"

"I do!" Raphael agreed.

Gabriel bent over the image in a state of awe. "It has been easy to forget that we were created to oversee this New Realm. In this, we can take comfort."

"Hear, hear!" Uriel cheered.

"I think it does no good to dwell on mysteries we cannot understand," Raphael said. "But this New Creation…now, here is something to hang our hopes on!"

Gabriel stood up from the ground and rolled

the paper into a neat scroll. Tucking it under his arm, he lifted his eyes toward the City Celeste, which was lost in the mists of heaven's highest level. His thoughts were far away, journeying through possibilities that might lie ahead.

When Michael interrupted his reveries, he was forced to consider the one possibility they feared most.

"Just for the sake of discussion," Michael said, "what if Lucifer is still alive? What if we must confront him again, someday? Will you all stand beside me, once more, as my generals?"

Gabriel stretched out his arms, embracing Raphael and Uriel on either side. "Michael, Who is Like the Lord without God's Comfort, God's Fire and God's Heroism? Of course we are with you!"

"That is what we were made for!" Uriel added.

"We were made to bring Glory to the Lord!" Raphael concluded.

Laughing together, the four locked arms, a band of brothers, and left the shattered halls of desecration. A New World lay ahead, and they meant to defend it at all costs.

Coming Soon!

Gabriel - God's Hero
Book II

GABRIEL
THE GRAND EXPERIMENT

**Contact your local bookstore or
visit <ellentraylor.com>**